PRAISE FOR

BUSH BLUES

"I met Sheldon when he was the chief in a small village in Western Alaska. Even then he had the gritty experience, quiet demeanor, and compassion that allows him to get into the head of Chief Snow and the steady rhythm of village life. *Bush Blues* marks the debut of an Alaskan crime solver as true and flawed as the state itself."

—Tom Begich, Alaska Senator

"*Bush Blues* is an exciting debut novel from Sheldon Schmitt. From page one he takes you on an Alaskan adventure of terrifying plane rides, deadly wildlife encounters, and most importantly humorous and delicately rendered character studies. Schmitt has put his thirty years of law enforcement experience and his big heart for the people he served to good use in this novel. *Bush Blues* is a terrific read."

—John Straley, Shamus winner and author of *Baby's First Felony*

BUSH BLUES

THE ADVENTURES OF
ALASKA'S POLICE CHIEF SNOW

SHELDON SCHMITT

VIRGINIA BEACH
CAPE CHARLES

Bush Blues:
The Adventures of
Alaska's Police Chief Snow

by Sheldon Schmitt

© Copyright 2018 Sheldon Schmitt

ISBN 978-1-63393-639-3

This is a work of fiction. The characters are both actual and fictitious. With the exception of verified historical events and persons, all incidents, descriptions, dialogue and opinions expressed are the products of the author's imagination and are not to be construed as real.

Published by

◄köehlerbooks™

210 60th Street
Virginia Beach, VA 23451
212-574-7939
www.koehlerbooks.com

A portion of the proceeds go to the Alaska Raptor Center in Sitka
alaskaraptor.org

DEDICATION

To Esther, Shelby, Steven and Sean.
Thanks for your love and support.

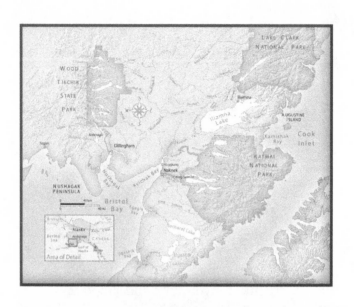

PROLOGUE

Chief Snow didn't see Buck Nelson until it was too late. Nelson barreled into Snow like a linebacker, driving the chief into the dirt. The chief lay stunned, feeling all of his old injuries.

Nelson had been wary of Snow ever since he showed up. He thought the police chief might suspect Nelson was up to no good. And there was no way Nelson was going to let this cop screw up his good thing. They were out in the middle of nowhere. No one around. *Easy to get rid of the body,* Nelson thought, *and tough to prove what happened.*

Nelson was a quick thinker. And bold—not afraid to act on instinct. It was why he had acted so nonchalant and congenial at first. Nelson wanted Snow to relax. And Snow did. The one advantage that bad guys had over other normal people was their willingness to kill without hesitation. Do the deed without stopping or remorse. Nelson had decided. It was just a matter of whether Snow was stupid or green enough to give him the opening. Once Nelson saw the chance, he did not hesitate. He was all in now; Snow was a dead man.

Snow hit the ground hard but instinctively rolled away. Nelson recovered quickly and scrambled back on top of Snow, grabbing for his throat. Snow squirmed and pushed with his legs, first one way and then the other, old wrestling moves that usually worked at getting out from under. But Nelson was strong and countered each move. The two tussled for what seemed to both like an eternity. Snow kept Nelson off his throat, but Nelson's power and size ground Snow down.

Snow bucked once, hard, got a little space, and slid his hand to release his weapon. He pulled the gun out, but Nelson knocked it loose and grabbed the chief's throat.

Snow began to panic and fought like a maniac as darkness crept into the corners of his vision. He grunted and wheezed as Nelson tightened his grip.

CHAPTER 1

THE CRASH

Togiak Police Chief Snow sat behind the only other passenger, Frank N Beans, in the white, battered Cessna Cherokee. The plane had a thin red stripe down the body and up the tail. Its single propeller was in front, with wings on the underside of the fuselage. The passengers and pilot had to clamber over the wings to gain entry through small, lightweight cabin doors, climbing on hands and knees, ass in the wind—a feat that often brought smiles to those waiting their turn.

The interior had tan faux-leather seats that had seen better days. The cabin doors had scratched Plexiglas windows, and they fastened shut with a latch at the top intended to make an airtight seal. But not in this case. The Cherokee hissed and moaned in flight as air wheezed through the door seals.

The plane held up to six people in rows of two with a small aisle in between. It had room for some freight and mail up in the nose and behind the passengers. The plane was very much like the pilot—a little haggard on the surface but competent underneath.

"Buckle up, girls. We're burning daylight!" shouted the pilot around the soggy stogie stump in the corner of his mouth.

"Eee! I am ready to go!" said Frank N Beans.

When he first came to Togiak, Chief Snow had struggled for months to understand the common Yupik expression, "Eee." He learned it was generally a form of acknowledgment or agreement. For example, if someone remarked that it was cold outside, a response of "eee" could mean "Yes, it's cold." But depending on the body language and inflection it could also mean "It's really cold!" or "Whatever."

Snow kept thinking he was missing nuances in the expression, but over time he accepted that sometimes things were just vague. It wasn't long before he used the term himself.

"No stops, straight through to Togiak," remarked Chubby to no one in particular.

Chubby, who was not all that chubby, taxied down the rough, checkered, snow-swept asphalt runway to face into the hard north wind. *Asphalt's much better than the usual bumpy, sand-and-rock runways in the bush,* Snow thought.

Chubby Libbet pulled the throttle back full as the plane was still turning into the wind. Snow's pulse quickened a little as the engine roared. He felt the vibrations in his bones and stomach. The familiar mix of excitement and anxiety took over as he looked into the threatening, gray sky to the west.

Flying in a small plane allowed solitude. The noise made it difficult to hear, so passengers mostly sat quietly, contemplating the scenery below and the integrity of the flying machine carrying them. And so it was for Snow. The chief smiled as he reminisced about his first flight in bush Alaska, which was piloted by one and the same Chubby. Snow relaxed as the plane bumped, creaked, and roared into the air before banking hard to the southwest, from Dillingham toward Togiak some eighty miles away over treeless, road-less wilderness.

The outskirts of Dillingham quickly passed. The land beneath was stark and stunning. Rolling hills and countless lakes and streams stretched in front of them, essentially untouched by humans. Despite the cold gray day, the view was awesome.

Snow thought back to when had first arrived in King Salmon on a jet ten years ago to the day, on his way to report to work at the wild and prodigious salmon fisheries of Bristol Bay. Snow was looking to make the big money. He had landed a job working for a cannery as a member of the "beach gang." It was a place to start. The real money was made on the fishing boats, or so he had heard. But working on the water was dangerous. Boats went down often enough that fishing was considered a high-risk occupation. But that didn't scare Snow off; in fact, that was the real reason he was there. Snow was drawn to the danger.

Somehow, he wound up on the wrong side of the Naknek River. The cannery where he had landed a job was on the other side of the Naknek River.

Young Snow screwed up the courage to ask for help. He needed to catch a ride across. He was directed to Chubby Libbit of Libbit's Flying Service in the summertime hustle and bustle of Naknek, a small fishing village whose population swelled with men working around the fishery.

Though it was getting late in the day, it was still light. In the Alaska summer the sun stayed up late and so did the people.

Snow knocked at the frame house next to a small runway of sand and rocks. The house was neatly painted white with red trim, similar to the famous pilot's whiskey-soaked eyeballs. The house appeared well kept with none of the usual array of junk, dead vehicles and animal carcasses that decorated the exterior of most homes in this area. Just the fact that it was neatly and fully painted was unusual. And bright white, no less. Snow timidly explained that he was looking for a ride across the river to the smaller village of South Naknek. There were no roads between the two Nakneks; you had to fly the mile or so over the mouth of the big brown Naknek River.

"Hey, maybe you want to take a boat across the river?" barked Chubby with a laugh. "Skinny, you remember that kid that tried to row across to see his sweetie? He ended up miles out to sea before someone picked him up, lucky he made it alive. The tides and current are fierce out here and nothing to mess with, son. Lots of boats have gone down in the Naknek River."

Most people flew in a bush plane across the river for routine business, despite the fact it was only a mile away. Bush planes were as common as taxies and used the same way. Children in remote villages rode planes to school.

Chubby invited Snow in for a drink as he finished his own warm whiskey with fellow bush pilot and drinker, Skinny, who was in fact skinny, with a beak of a nose. Snow was pleased to be offered a drink. He felt a little less apprehensive and not quite so young.

At that time, Snow was eighteen years old. Although he was raised in Alaska, this was his first experience out on his own. His adopted parents were not thrilled about his Alaska adventure. Bristol Bay had kind of a Wild West reputation, even by Alaskan standards. But Snow was determined to go. He was itching to get away from home and out on his own.

Skinny was a great bush pilot in his own right, but Chubby was the star of the show, or most any act in which he was a player.

Chubby wore a blue captain's hat with scrambled eggs on the brim. He wore the hat at about the same angle he sauntered, which was a tilted, John Wayne at Rio Bravo bravado stride. He talked around a half-chewed cigar that was as much a part of his appearance as his hat, which Snow never saw Chubby without.

And here he was again, gumming a cigar and piloting Snow.

As they flew south, Snow realized he had never seen Chubby actually *smoke* a cigar. If anything, he manically masticated those soggy stogies and, really, you didn't want to look too close anyway. But he was a hilarious bullshitter full of the devil and demon rum. He could make most folks laugh just by showing up and saying something, anything—even those who did not particularly like him for some reason or another, and those people were around, to be sure.

Chubby had a widespread reputation as one of the best bush pilots that ever jerked a stick, and he had flair, to boot. He was the antithesis of the old saying, "There are old pilots and there are bold pilots, but there are no old, bold pilots." Although he knew these parts, he wasn't from this raw country.

Chubby was a white man of mostly Irish blood who had the look of an Irishman. He was ruddy in the face and nose and not a large man at all. But he seemed large because of his confidence and manner. He had a twinkle in his eye and a wry smile when not chewing a cigar. His hair was a reddish-brown wiry mop under his hat, with a couple white and gray hairs mixed in. Most of the time he wore jeans and a brown bomber jacket that was worn white at the shoulders and elbows. He almost always wore dark brown, leather deck slippers in the summer.

The fact that he was a hard drinker did nothing to diminish his reputation as a pilot. In those rough days in the bush, he was an aviation pioneer. His reputation was surely enhanced by his affinity for the drink and his ability to handle it. Hard drinking was part of the culture.

Snow remembered fondly that first meeting with Chubby and how no adult had ever offered him a drink before. He remembered that offer of a drink made Snow feel a little braver and just a little more of a man.

That night years ago, no adult had ever offered him a drink before. Snow listened to Chubby and Skinny trade lies while they drank until Chubby suddenly turned to Snow with a bark.

"We're burning daylight! Grab yer gear, boy!"

Snow startled to life, shouldered his beat-up green seabag, and hustled to keep up with the side-winding Chubby, who led him out to an off-white Cessna 206.

Chubby fiddled around for a few seconds and fired the plane up, wasting no time in barreling down the short gravel-and-rock runway on spongy tundra tires. Rocks smacked ominously on the underside of the plane. Chubby took off with the wind and headed right across the river into a thick fog. They were flying blind.

"Don't worry, kid! The fog usually hangs on the river. It'll clear on the other side."

And, sure enough, it did. Chubby dropped the plane down and came in right over the river bank, about forty feet above a house that Snow later learned was occupied by the cannery superintendent. The super's name was Odd Snortstad, and his personality fit the name. Right over the house, Chubby pulled the throttle back and forth, revving the engine to buzz the super and let him know he had a passenger to pick up at the airport. Chubby laughed and barked, "That always drives old Odd crazy."

The buzzing always seemed to startle Odd, who would spit out a couple curse words before smiling about it. But the super was enchanted with Chubby like most people and put up with the local pilot's rude and flamboyant ways. What was he going to do about it anyway?

Chief Snow reminisced about working at the cannery for a man named Odd. *Lots of odd names, or nicknames, in those days. It was different then,* he thought. *Wilder or newer or something.*

Snow worked with a friend everyone called "Delirious," a fellow from Bozeman called "Montana," a guy from, well, somewhere, who they stuck with the nickname of "Crib Death." And "Wild Bill" from Ohio was wild whether he was drinking or not. *Such characters.*

■ ■ ■

The plane finally warmed up about twenty minutes into the hour-or-so ride to Togiak. The vibration, engine hum, and gathering warmth made Snow sleepy as he watched the snow-swept tundra and frozen lakes pass a thousand feet below. Snow looked out the starboard window over the wing. Off to the northwest, he could see the foothills of the low-slung Wood River Mountains and a series of large, deep lakes renowned for their excellent fishing. A dirt road led from Dillingham to the first lake in the chain, but after that you had to access the lakes by boat or floatplane. The lakes of the Tikchik State Park were a destination for avid and well-funded sport fisherman. World-class rainbow trout and dollies awaited those who made the trip.

Directly below were miles upon miles of flat, brown, road-less lowlands dotted with a seemingly endless array of lakes. The winds blew like the devil out there, and the snow was swept clean except where it found a place to catch. There was hardly a sign of human existence. Snow machine trails were visible as they left the metropolis of Dillingham, the hub city with about twenty-five hundred people. But the trails soon petered out and then the vista below appeared untouched. Snow spied a puny shack beside one of the larger lakes and wondered about the people who built it. *Why? And how?* He imagined the hardy souls hauling materials and tools so far off the grid to build a simple shack. He wondered if he could do that.

Frank N Beans dozed in front of Snow. Suddenly, Chubby steered the plane down at a steep angle. He banked around and barked something back at Beans and Snow, but Snow could not hear what he was saying. Snow could tell by the excited barking and cigar chomping that Chubby had spotted something and they were going down for a look. Chubby spiraled the plane down until they had done a 360 and were retracing their path, closer to the ground. Chubby wagged the wings back and forth and buzzed an unsuspecting brown bear below.

"Look at that sumbitch!" Chubby yelled.

Snow saw the brown bear as they were bearing down on it. It was on its hind legs and clawing at the air to swat the noisy intruder. Snow winced as they passed over. The bear stood over ten feet tall. Chubby laughed and barked.

Frank N Beans said something to Snow, revealing a gap-toothed smile under his thick black mustache. Beans's speech, a wonder to understand even under ideal conditions, was impossible now, so Snow smiled and raised his eyebrows in agreement, as was the custom.

Like the expression "Eee," raising one's eyebrows was a common means of communication with the Yupik. Raising both eyebrows usually meant "yes" or "I understand." When he first arrived, Snow asked a local man a question several times. The man did not answer; he just kept looking at Snow with a look of surprise. Snow realized later that he *had* been responding. Snow had simply not understood that his look of surprise was him saying "yes" with his eyebrows.

Frank N Beans fiddled around, getting comfortable again. Snow did the same as he thought about Beans. *Frank N Beans is the reason for this trip to town in the first place, dammit,* thought Snow. He had arrested him the night before and, after leaving Frank overnight in one of the two cells at the station, ended up transporting him to Dillingham for arraignment. *What a goat rope.*

Beans was gentle and often unintelligible. He stood about five foot two in his white, rubber bunny boots and rarely got violent. When he did, he was usually drunk, which he often was. Snow had once seen him with a black eye from a skirmish with his brother, Stanley Beans, who had also been drunk as usual. But violence was an anomaly for the Beans boys. Frank was quiet in his ways and smiled a lot. He was small-boned and dark-skinned with a flat face. His head seemed too big and square for his body. His legs were so bowed that his bones looked curved. He walked in the side-to-side manner of a person who worked on the water all his life, making him look drunk even when he was less so. His eyebrows shot up all the time, which could mean just about anything. The natives in this country were very expressive with their eyebrows, Frank N Beans, more than most. His bobbed like a skiff at anchor in the wind.

But last night something had snapped in Beans. Frank had picked up a shotgun, staggered next door and shot his neighbor's dog, which was chained in front of the house. Double-aught buckshot speckled the front of the house. He then got on a snow machine and roared off. The police chief was called to keep the peace. It was dark and snowing as Chief Snow drove to that side of town. He got flagged down by Johnny Ahnaungatogurauk—or "Johnny A-through-K," as everyone called him.

Johnny A-through-K was pretty shook up as he described how Beans had tipped his snow machine over by the post office. When A through K stooped to check on Beans's condition, he looked down the barrel of the shotgun. Beans did not shoot him, but clearly A through K felt like he had dodged death. Frank N Beans had mumbled something and lurched off to the east, toward his house.

Chief Snow followed Beans's trail to his house easy enough. Snow could have called the troopers in, but they wouldn't have made it until at least the next day, by which time either someone would be dead, or Frank would be passed out and sobering up. Snow had parked his junkie Ford F250 pickup back by the post office. He approached the house to see if he could talk to Frank. He stood off to the side of the entry, where he could peek around the corner and see the front windows.

Chief Snow banged on the side of the house. The windows

were dark and there was no sound from within. He was already getting chilly; it was probably twenty below or so. The snow crunched underfoot, a nuisance, bad for trying to be sneaky. The bright snow made it seem lighter out.

He kicked the house, scattering snow and making enough noise to be sure it could be heard or felt. The snowflakes swirled prettily around Chief Snow's face. He was glad he paid the extra money for the Danner steel-toe boots, which were excellent for kicking on doors. It was usually too cold to knock with your bare hand, and pounding on the door wearing heavy gloves just made muffled thumps. The boot was the thing.

Snow peered around the corner and hollered, "Frank, it's Chief Snow. I need to talk to you."

Snow was surprised to see Beans crank open the large window in the kitchen. Beans had no shirt on as he said, "Sheef Shnow! What cher doing?"

There was no sign of the violence described by Johnny earlier. That did not surprise Snow much. This was the great alcohol enigma. Anyway, it seemed like Beans was back to normal, though drunk.

Chief Snow tried to convince Beans to come to the door. As drunk as he was, Beans seemed to understand that if he came to the door it might not be a good thing for him. But Snow gently coaxed him out, mostly by simply not going away. Beans came out barefoot, wearing only loose black denim jeans. Snow talked to him about what happened. Beans seemed clueless and unable to understand what was going on.

When Snow gave him the bad news that he was going to have to accompany Snow, Beans said, "Eee! Sheef."

Snow helped him slip on a parka, some white bunny boots, and some handcuffs, which all took a little time because Beans wanted to hug Snow and was now crying about something. Everything was fine until right at the jail cell door. Beans realized where he was and suddenly began to fight. Snow had to wrestle him down to the floor. Beans was surprisingly strong for his size, slobbering and slurring. Snow had learned the hard way in the past not to underestimate a drunk. Snow got him prone, made a dash for the cell door, and got it shut before Beans banged into it. Snow was so relieved to have everyone safe he did not even mind that Beans hollered, wailed, cursed, and sobbed for a couple hours before passing out.

In the morning Frank was sober and very apologetic. Chief Snow explained the sorry events of the night before, including the tussle they had in the cell.

"You know, I am kind of sore after rolling around on the ground with you, Frank. Surprised, too. We never had any problems in the past, you and me."

Beans said he was sorry and seemed to mean it. He told Snow that he had a couple jugs of booze and did not remember what had happened. Snow explained to him the charges and opened the cell. Snow and Beans ate microwave sausage-and-cheese muffins, which were actually pretty good. *Not as good as McDonald's,* thought Snow, *but almost.* Frank had never had an Egg McMuffin in his life, and he thought it was good. Snow made some fresh coffee and they sat at his desk drinking out of chipped, off-white ceramic cups.

Snow explained the charges again, and Beans's rights. Beans worried about what was going to happen with the judge or magistrate at the arraignment. Usually arraignments were held right there at Snow's beat-up metal desk, over the speakerphone with the ancient Magistrate Sadie Neakok. This could be a real problem at times, what with the crappy connection and echoes bouncing off the satellite phone links. Magistrate Neakok was known not to mince words but also for being tough but fair.

But this was a felony, and Beans had to appear in person at the courthouse in Dillingham. Snow told Beans that he would explain to the magistrate how the incident was out of character for Beans. The chief would see if he could get Beans released on the condition that Frank refrained from drinking.

■ ■ ■

In the courtroom, old Sadie shamed Beans to the point where it looked like he might cry. The magistrate sternly said, "Mr. Frank N Beans, I am ashamed of you! Your father was a whaling captain, God rest his soul. He would be ashamed of you, too!"

Even though Beans had it coming, Snow felt sorry for him. Neakok was tougher than walrus meat. She was seventy-something, knew everyone, and had seen it all. She knew the problems associated with the demon rum but did not tolerate fools or drunks.

Magistrate Neakok was respected and feared, though she was all of five foot nothing and maybe 120 pounds with her parkie and mukluks. She was sharp as a tack and had bright, bouncing eyes in her wrinkled brown face. She wore a nice set of dentures in court, but she was not shy about going without when she was at home. She was spry and would talk your leg off if you ran into her at the house. When she was done talking, she would get up and walk away. If you did not know any better, you might think she was coming back, but she had already dismissed you and would be surprised if you were still sitting there when and if she did return.

Magistrate Neakok asked Chief Snow for his recommendations, which was the ritual. She listened to Snow despite his being a relative *cheechako*, or "newcomer," to Togiak. Snow knew the history of the folks in town, tried to work with the people he arrested if he could, and he did not needlessly stack charges.

"Frank N Beans does not normally behave like this," Snow told the magistrate. "He has no history of violent crime. His mother, Lima Beans, has a bad leg. She depends on Frank and his brother to care for her. Normally, I would not recommend an OR release for a crime this serious, but I am this time. I recommend Frank N Beans be released to the third-party custody of his mother, Lima, or his brother, Stanley, and that he check in every morning for a breath test."

Frank was sobbing now, which was about to get Chief Snow going too. He knew that old Lima Beans needed Frank. As long as he stayed sober, Snow figured it would be all right. The daily morning breath test had worked pretty well in the past. And so it went. Neakok released Beans on felony gun charges based on the recommendation of the chief of police. *What the hell,* thought Snow. *I must be stupid or crazy. I hope the Dillingham cops or troopers don't hear about this.* In his heart, he felt he had done the right thing—a good thing.

■ ■ ■

The engine sputtered, pulling Snow back from his reverie. Or maybe he imagined the engine sputter. It was better not to think about it, Snow had learned. *You're dead meat, anyway, if you do go down, so why worry?*

Everyone who lived out in the bush flew all the time. You could tough it out on a snow machine for a dozen or more bone-jarring hours, which was exhausting and dangerous. In the summer, you could take a boat around the coast, but people seldom did unless to get some major work done to their boat in Dillingham. No, flying was the only real way to get around out here.

When Snow was younger, he thought crashing was a one-in-a-million shot, so the odds were high. Problem was the odds seemed to get whittled down after years of flying.

He heard the plane sputter for sure and looked intently at Chubby, who was suddenly deadly serious. Chubby talked into the mouthpiece of the pea-green headphones he wore over his blue captain's hat. Chubby did not look back at the passengers. Best not to make eye contact in these situations. It was beginning to snow, and flakes peeled off above and below the wing. They were gradually descending from the thousand or so feet that Chubby had climbed after buzzing the big brown bear.

The engine sputtered and stopped.

Shocked surprise.

Silence.

Wind whistling through the cracks around the cabin doors.

Chubby tried to restart the engines. No luck. While he worked at the controls, he was also busy peering over the high dash of the Cherokee. Snow's mind was suddenly racing. He thought stupidly that he always wondered why they had such a shitty design that the pilot could barely see over the dash. *What kind of fucked up engineering was that?* Then Snow saw what Chubby saw: a frozen lake ahead of them. Chubby was apparently going to try and make the lake and put her down there before they hit the ground.

Chubby hollered around his cigar, "Hang on, boys!" His voice boomed in the quiet cabin. "We're going down!"

Chubby was chewing the cigar like mad, eyes moving rapidly back and forth like a dog looking for scraps, his skinny butt barely touching the seat as he leaned over the dash of the little plane. *We're not going to make it,* thought Snow. *We're goners if we hit the tundra.*

Planes that crashed in the tundra usually cracked up. The tundra was not flat and rolling like it looked from the air, like the plains of the Midwest. It was very rough in spots, with what the locals called muskeg. Such it looked to be here, which meant it would be lucky if they did not flip or simply crash into one of the soft-looking crags stuck five feet in the air. Snow thought they would never make it—but then hope. Crazy, wild hope! He began to think Chubby might pull it off. *If anyone can, it's Chubby, all right; he had the luck of the Irish!* He certainly looked the part.

The plane was eerily quiet as it dropped lower and lower. Suddenly they were over the ice and the wheels touched down. The plane hopped and touched down again. The wheels hit a snowdrift and the plane lurched forward, causing the propeller to hit the ice. The plane bobbed back on its wheels but had gotten off line and went into a slow spin, sliding through the drifts. Everyone on board waited for the plane to crash or flip. But it didn't; it just stopped.

And then there was quiet.

CHAPTER 2
THE BEAR

"**G**oddamn it! That was a new prop!" Chubby huffed.

"Not anymore," remarked Frank N Beans with such clarity that Chubby and the chief turned to see if it was really Frank N Beans who made that remark. Beans's eyebrows bobbed under his heavy black bangs. He had a grin stuck on his mouth.

"Huh?" said Chubby.

We made it. We're alive, ya crazy fuckers! Snow thought.

Chubby knew they were lucky to be alive but was already moving onto the next thing. He still had his cigar in his mouth, which suddenly seemed hilarious to Snow. But Beans felt the need to commemorate their good fortune with a loud, garbled pronouncement and a fist pump.

Chubby muttered and scrambled forward, crawling out of the plane onto the wing and down onto the ice. He slipped but caught himself on the aileron, remaining upright.

There were drifts and patches of snow on the unnamed lake,

which was about two miles across and fairly round.

An estimated three million lakes were in the Alaskan wilderness, scattered like raindrops by a reckless God. But only about three thousand of those lakes had been named, mostly the very big or remarkable ones. They were primarily known only by their longitude and latitude numbers. They were a spot on a map, a reference point for some other destination.

Clean spots on the surface of the lake were so windswept that they could see the smooth ice. Chief Snow crawled out of the plane through the pilot's door right behind Beans, who was mumbling.

Once on the ice, Snow looked down at his boots. *Great for kicking doors, but not good for extended time out of doors.* Frank N Beans wore a white, canvas over-parka with a wolf ruff around the hood and hands, typical attire for locals who hunted, which was most of the men and boys. Beans also had some mittens and the same white bunny boots he wore when he was arrested the night before. He looked perfectly natural and comfortable in the snow and dying light. Snow slipped and slid back to the rear of the plane, ready for Chubby to hand things out.

The light faded ominously. The snow came down harder, though at least the wind was not blowing much. Chubby assessed the situation.

"I activated the emergency locator transmitter. That means they will know we had a problem right quick like. I've got some survival gear and first aid kit back here."

Snow peeked around Chubby and saw a jug of whiskey and a five-pound bag of dog food that apparently constituted the survival gear. There were also matches, black plastic trash bags, a can opener and a few other small assorted items in the canvas sack. Snow had seen the bag of puppy chow before, several times, and now asked Chubby about it.

"You got a puppy, Chubby?" Snow said, pointing at the bag.

"Nah, that's my survival food. I used to always throw some

food like candy bars and jerky in the tail, but it seemed like it would always disappear. Kids got to it, I suppose," said Chubby. "Anyways, I got the idea of the dog food. It's actually supposed to be good for you, and nobody's gonna eat it lest they're really starving."

Snow wasn't so sure about it being good for you but agreed no one would be eager to dig into it.

As if reading his mind, Frank grumbled, "Eee, I'm not eating that shit."

Better hide that whiskey, Chubby, thought Snow. *Frank does not need the temptation.*

"You'll eat it if you get hungry enough, Frank. Trust me," Chubby said.

Snow took a personal inventory. He had his sidearm. And he had a Leatherman tool. He also had his radio, but they were out of range of anywhere and everybody. *No cell phone, but no coverage anyway.* He had no food or water, of course.

Snow always figured that he would die if he were ever in a crash, so he never bothered packing a survival kit. It was only by chance that he was dressed as warmly as he was. He wore blue overalls and a blue parka with a nice wolf ruff. This was Snow's normal attire when on duty, and neither he or his prisoner had packed anything extra for the trip.

Snow considered whether to stay with the downed plane. But there was no heat on a dead plane and they would freeze. The better bet was to find shelter on land.

The emergency locator transmitter (ELT) had its own battery, so it was able to send out a distress signal. But it was an older model without precise GPS coordinates to transmit, so searchers would only have a general idea of where to look. The weather was less than ideal for a search effort as dark descended and the snow picked up. *I wonder if they will even launch until morning,* he thought. *But even the Coast Guard ought to be able to find us on a frozen lake.*

"What do you think, Chubby? Stay with the plane?" he asked.

"We'll freeze out here. There's a hunting cabin on the south side of this lake. I've seen it from the air. I ain't that sure exactly where it is, but we outta be able to find her. If we stay here we'll freeze harder than dog turds most likely!"

Beans started walking—sliding, really—bowlegged, to the south.

"Find a cabin. Easy shit," he said. "Follow me."

"Frank! You sure you know the way?" Snow hollered. He slipped and fell on the ice as he started after Beans, who looked back at Chubby and Snow like they were stupid, waving his arm for them to follow.

"Well shit, Chief! Looks like Frank's our guide. Good thing you arrested him! Ha ha!" Chubby said, apparently looking on the bright side of things.

Frank N Beans was no guide, but he had lived and hunted in the bush his entire life. Neither Chubby nor Snow questioned him; they simply followed and hoped he knew what he was doing.

If Frank had not gotten shit-faced drunk and done a bunch of idiotic violent things to get arrested for, would have never had to make this trip in the first place, Snow thought.

Chubby shouldered the canvas bag and set out after Beans, heading into the unknown. *If we live through this, I'll be even more famous,* thought Chubby. *They will talk about us at the Sea Inn Bar in Dillingham for a long time, because there is not that much to talk about in the wintertime at the bar—at least not in bush Alaska, anyway.*

Chief Snow put his hood up and fell in behind as they slide-walked single file toward the south side of the unnamed lake about forty air miles from the nearest town. It was the tail end of winter as early night fell.

They made the side of the lake about the time it was getting dark. The snow was still coming down, but it did not seem to be getting any colder. They said snow could actually warm air temperatures in Alaska.

Snow looked ahead at his mates. Beans appeared in his element; Chubby was too indomitable to get cold. *Only I am cold,* thought Snow. *I am the weak one.* He resolved that the words "I am cold" would never come out of his mouth, even if his lips were frozen blue.

Suddenly, the chief felt a push from behind, a forceful shove that knocked him down. *What the hell?* Before he could turn he heard the snort and growl. A massive brown bear stood leering.

Snow hoped that they had startled the bear and it would simply run off into the night. That's what bears usually did, after all. They didn't want anything to do with humans, but they could be unpredictable beasts. Sometimes they charged for no apparent reason.

Snow watched in horror as the bear wheeled with awful majesty, snow swirling up like a tempest and partially obscuring the beautiful but lethal beast. The big brown behemoth charged, grunting and huffing and making unworldly noises, its eyes fixed on the chief. Snow thought he heard the bear's claws scrape the lake ice. He lay frozen, and then the bear was on top of him.

The bear pummeled Snow with blows to his upper body. Huge, strong arms, nothing like a man's at all. Snow felt the breeze and heard the swoosh the big arms made as they pummeled him. Paralyzed with fear, he saw the terrible creature's fur up close through the fur of his parka. It was like looking at a rug come crazily alive. He thought absently that the thick fur *really* would make a good rug. Wild, stupid thoughts in the middle of a mauling.

The bear bit his shoulder and ripped and bit again. Ferocious snapping. Snow heard the jaws snap, the cloth of his coat rip, and the deep guttural noises from deep inside the bear. Spit flew from the bear's hellacious maw as the jaws worked. The bear made a primeval grunting noise no man would ever want to hear up close. Snow played dead, a ploy often used in bear attacks. It was his only defense.

Frank and Chubby had done what was only natural when a bear charges—run in terror. As they slipped away, they heard the bear mauling Snow. Better to wait until it left.

Snow sucked his shoulder away from the bear. He was lucky so far; the bear was getting mostly clothing in its mouth. His head was in the parka and had not been bitten, yet. The bear swiped Snow hard, slower this time, as if toying with him. *Left. Right. Left.* One swipe ripped his overalls, raked his flesh, and drew some blood. Snow was dazed. The whole thing seemed like it was happening in slow motion. He smelled the breath of the ten-foot bear. It felt *hot* and malicious. Time slowed almost to a stop.

Then the bear seemed satisfied, suddenly slowing its attack and pausing. It batted Snow a couple times and bit him again, almost half-heartedly. Snow's hand was at his side. He had a thought like a revelation straight from heaven, from God himself.

Gun! His gun was by his hand. He slid his hand down and unsnapped the holster in one smooth motion. *Point-blank range. Can't miss*, thought Snow. He pulled the trigger once, twice, three times, and then again. Snow could not hear the gun but could see the flash. It was odd. He smelled the distinctive and pleasant odor of the gunfire, and then burning hair.

The bear's roar shook Chief Snow to his roots. A roar from hell. He swore later he could feel the hot fetid breath of the bear. The bear wheeled away and ran. Snow emptied his magazine wildly at the scurrying beast. He lowered the gun as the bear disappeared into the snowy horizon, and he passed out.

■ ■ ■

Snow came to. He did not know how long he had been out. He awoke shivering, frozen to the bone. He checked himself over, felt his injuries. *This is really bad. So stupid. All three of us so manically happy to be alive we forgot about the big bear we just buzzed a few minutes ago. What the hell was the bear doing out and about anyway? And why did it charge? No cubs to protect this time of year.*

It was winter and the brown bears were supposed to be hibernating. *Just pure bad luck, plain and simple.* Sometimes they would come out in the winter but not for very long. *Just bad luck,* thought Snow again.

He struggled to his feet and checked his body. His injuries were painful. His left shoulder felt like it had bled some—his thigh, too. He could tell he was bruised and battered, but he was lucky; with all the clothing he was wearing, his body had not gotten too ripped up. *Lucky that the bear did not bite my head,* he thought. That was how most people died. When the bear was big enough to get his jaws around their head and bite down, the bear would crush the person's skull. *Such pleasant thoughts I have today,* he thought absently, acidly.

Chief Snow wondered about Chubby and Beans. He imagined that they simply lit out when the bear charged. He wondered how far they got and hoped they made it to the cabin and didn't get split up from each other.

Snow wondered if he had shot the bear. He was pretty sure he hit him, but he could not see any blood. It was still snowing, so maybe the blood trail was covered up. A wounded bear was a dangerous bear, so he might return.

Snow pulled the ripped clothing on his thigh closer. His feet were going numb. His fingers, too. He curled his toes inside his boot, but it was painful. He gingerly took some steps. *Got to get moving, keep moving.* He walked and limped in the direction he thought Chubby and Beans had been heading, looking for some sign of their trail. He saw what he thought were impressions in the snow but was not sure. There was a lot of bare ice with no sign of tracks. He spotted the bear trail but definitely did not want to go that way. It was now almost dark, and the snow was driving down hard.

Chief Snow was lost and freezing. His ears had been frostbitten before so were now more susceptible to it, even though he had his hood; they got the familiar burning feeling. He tried not to think about it, but he could not feel his feet. They were like blocks of wood. His feet had been frostbitten mildly before, too, so he was used to the feeling of no feeling.

He called out for Chubby and Beans, but his voice seemed to evaporate in the snowflakes.

Snow made it into a stand of scrub pine trees on the lake's edge. He sat on a small fallen log and decided to smoke. *What the hell.* He still had his smokes and lighter, a small miracle. *Maybe my last smoke,* he thought. He was at a loss for what to do. *Try to start a fire?* If he could find the plane, he could set *that* on fire. A big, huge hot fire. *Nothing to do but go on. Keep moving, don't stop moving.* Except he was so tired. He finished his smoke and wondered if he should just fall asleep there for a while. *Is that what happens?* he thought. *Is this how people freeze to death? They just go to sleep? Not a bad way to go,* he supposed, but he was not ready to lay down. Not quite yet. It was a close decision and needed a little more thought.

Suddenly he heard a voice.

"Hey, laddie. Come on, now, don't be giving up."

Snow was eye to eye with a strange man, despite the fact that Snow was sitting down. The elfish little fellow had an old-fashioned kerosene lantern, and he instructed Snow to get up and follow him, waving to him. *Strange I did not see him coming,* thought Snow.

"Are you with the Coast Guard?" he asked, instantly regretting the stupid remark.

The little man instead stated that Snow had shot and killed

the bear. Well, it was not dead yet but was going to die for certain. It was dying, the little man said. The tiny fellow had an English accent, which somehow fit his bizarre appearance. Snow thought he must be a Native who studied at Oxford or something crazy. *Why not? Makes about as much sense as the rest of this day.*

Snow slowly got to his feet. He realized belatedly that he never reloaded his sidearm. For some reason he needed to do it now. He loaded a fresh magazine and slid the gun back into his holster, fumbling with the snap because his fingers were made of stone. He took one step and then another, following the stranger.

The little man led the way through the scrub pines, alder bushes, and tundra. The trees were very short and sickly in this area. This part of western Alaska was mostly devoid of trees, the large open country covered by grass or tundra and populated by migrating herds of caribou numbering in the tens of thousands. This was the country of brown bears grown enormous on the millions of salmon that plugged every creek and river to spawn. A county so big and open it spoke to the very souls of men.

The little man led Chief Snow through the pine trees to the south side of a hill. There was a ravine that looked to be made from runoff. Up in the ravine the little man went. A small, very old-looking cabin appeared in front of them. It was hard to see in the dark and snowy night. Snow struggled to make it up the short climb.

The man opened the door into the one-room cabin, which looked simple and small and dark. The gnomish stranger set his lamp on a crude table made of two-by-fours with an ancient piece of plywood on top. He quickly started a fire in the old barrel stove at the back. Snow sat on a small plywood bunk and watched his host work as the room warmed up. Snow looked around, but there was not much to see—a couple cupboards. He did not bother to look in them; he was bone-tired.

"What is your name?" Snow asked. He wanted to express his

gratitude and really wanted to do so by name.

The man seemed to ignore Snow as he dug inside his pack. In the dim light of the cabin, Snow noticed that his host was not carrying a gun of any kind. His cloak was made of what looked to be stitched wolf hide. Underneath the fur cloak was a finer garment that appeared to be intricately hand-sewn out of tanned caribou hide. The man also wore a pair of the nicest mukluks Snow had ever seen. They looked to have a seal hide on the bottom with sealskin up to his short knees. The clothing looked Native to Snow, but not all from this region. He had only seen comparable clothing on display at a museum or worn during a Native ceremony, such as a feast after the whaling season.

Snow was musing about these things as the small man turned to address him.

"You call me Kinka," he said in his strange accent.

"I heard that before. Isn't *kinka* Yupik for 'love'?" asked Snow.

Kinka seemed pleased by Snow's question—a smile stretched his wide mouth.

Kinka said, "Aye, my name could indeed mean 'love' in Yupik. But it could also mean 'like,' 'benevolence' or 'kindness.' I was given the name of *Kinka* by tribal members of the Yupik Natives some years ago as sign of favor, or like a tribute from them. Chief Wasillie the elder told me that because I had bestowed kindness to their clan, they would call me Kinka."

Snow was intrigued by this information and had questions. But first he needed to say thanks.

"Kinka, I want to thank you for saving my life. I would have frozen if not for you. I feel bad about killing the bear, though. It was my fault, I suppose, for not paying attention. I'm Chief Snow, from Togiak. Thank you, Kinka. *Quyana*." Snow said the last in Yupik. He felt like he might suddenly cry, overcome with emotion.

Kinka held Snow's gaze for a few seconds and seemed to

take the measure of him before going back to his bag. Snow noticed with interest that Kinka was preparing food—caribou meat, it looked like.

"That bear came out of its cave a bit early. He was hungry and nearly blind. If you had been paying attention, you could have possibly avoided the bear. But maybe not; hard to be sure. The bear might have smelled you and decided to hunt you down. One thing is sure: your meeting with this bear was destiny.

"I don't think ye wanted to kill the bear, but expect ye had no choice, as you are not ready to die. This bear was put into your life for some reason, I think. It is up to you, Chief, to seek the meaning of the bear. And to give thanks for its life. I like yer name, Snow. It fits ye," Kinka said with a twinkle.

"My birth mother named me that. So, I was told by my adopted parents," said Snow. "I'm really not sure about that. I never met my real mom."

"Ye should meet her. Ye should know your mother."

Snow slumped back and unzipped his coat. He had the sensation of being out of his body. Everything seemed off kilter, but the warm cabin felt like heaven. His fingers were burning and red; he thought that was a good sign. He slowly rubbed his hands together. They were vaguely itchy. His ears and his toes burned, but at least he could feel his feet. Snow untied his boots and removed them, rubbing his feet through his wool socks, but what felt good for his hands hurt his feet.

His shoulder throbbed and he tried not to move. His legs hurt too. He was in sorry shape as he dozed off.

He woke up to the smell of food. Kinka was in front of him telling him to sit up. Kinka mischievously tapped Snow's forehead with a wooden spoon. Snow shrugged off his coat and sat up. During the short nap his shoulder and legs had stiffened up and were aching. Kinka said he wanted to take a look at Snow's injuries. Snow agreed and stripped off his layers. It was a painful and slow process. He finally got down to the fourth and final layer, his blue T-shirt, and hesitated before taking it off. Snow had always been shy about that sort of thing.

Snow was down to his skivvies. He had fairly deep wounds above his knee, but they had not bled much. One good thing about the cold—it slowed the bleeding. The wounds were the type that anybody could identify as claw marks.

Kinka examined Snow's left shoulder while the chief chewed on caribou meat. Snow was interested to see the damage, too, which amounted to a lot of indentations and several punctures from the bear's teeth. But there had not been much blood as the punctures were not deep. The indentations were turning dark blue and the general area was very red, boasting an impressive set of claw marks. The main problem was the possibility of infection, a broken bone or some deep bruising.

"Nothing broken," Kinka declared.

"Looks like I'll have some impressive scars," Snow said.

"Seen lots worse," Kinka said. "Gots a few of me own."

Kinka dug into his bag again and extracted some strange items. He took Snow's T-shirt and wetted it in a wooden bowl of water sitting on the rickety table. Kinka quickly cleaned Snow's wounds with the water, which also seemed to contain antiseptic. Kinka's movements were quick and sure.

"How did you find me?" asked Snow.

"Was out checkin' traps. I saw ye fight the bear. I thought ye vood lose!" He spread greenish herbal paste on the gash and deep scratches on Snow's thigh and put what was left on Snow's shoulder. Kinka fetched caribou stew from a pot and handed Snow a bowl. There were no eating utensils, so Snow got out his Leatherman. Kinka looked at it with interest and Snow handed it to him.

"Try it out, Kinka," Snow said to the little man. As Snow sipped from the bowl, Kinka manipulated the tool with his slender, dexterous brown fingers. Kinka looked bemused as he opened the various implements and blades.

Snow's mind felt overwrought by the cataclysmic events of this long day. He was not sure what was real or not, whether to trust his mind and senses. He fished out a chunk of caribou from the broth and chewed it slowly as he watched the miniature, enigmatic man named Kinka, with the odd clothing and accent and mysterious ways, play with his Leatherman in the soft lamplight. Snow could not judge his age; Kinka looked beyond age, as if from another time.

"Can you tell me why Elder Wasillie gave you the name of Kinka? And what do your people call you?" Snow asked.

Asking the question, it occurred to him that he was sure Kinka was not a Yupik Eskimo, though he felt sure of nothing else at the moment.

"When the men in the whaling boats first came to this region, many Natives became sick and died. It was mostly the smallpox. I helped the Natives and the elders to deal with the sickness, death, and grief. It was indeed a very sad time, a difficult time. I think they were grateful for any help. I did little enough," said Kinka with a far-off look in his eyes. "I have interacted with many people over time and had other names. And I thought Chief Wasillie was a wise man."

Snow focused on the way Kinka said "people" like he was not one of them or they were different from him, and he finally understood. Kinka was one of the "Little People." Snow had heard tales and talk of them but thought them fictional folklore. Now he was sure he was dreaming or dead.

Kinka continued, "My name means 'One who is tossed by the wind.' They call me that because I like to move around; I am a drifter. I learned to speak yer language from a man named Captain Shoemaker, who I met near to here. The captain's boat had gotten iced in, and they had to stay the winter. The captain had been inland hunting for food when he got separated from his party and lost in a snowstorm. Captain Shoemaker told me he came on the whaling boat from a place called England. He was a good man, and filled with many thoughts and ideas. But not too good out in the wilderness, getting lost like that. He was like yerself, Chief Snow."

"What are the Little People, Kinka?" Chief Snow asked, taking a chance. Kinka's easy answer confirmed Snow's hunch.

"We are like ye but not. I guess I would say we are closer to the spirit world, and yer closer to the earth," said Kinka. "Now ye need to lay back and sleep, recover."

Snow felt drugged. He pulled on some clothing and used his lumpy parka as a blanket. He felt warm and good despite the adventurous day, injuries, and nagging feeling of uneasiness, like nothing was as it seemed. He fell into a deep sleep.

CHAPTER 3
THE RESCUE

Snow woke up. He heard snow crunching under foot and muffled voices growing louder as they approached the cabin, which was dark except for light coming through the chinks in the log walls and under the rough-hewn plank door. The door burst open and in came Trooper Dickron, followed by his partner, Trooper Debbie Roop. Snow was very happy to see them, and they were happy and relieved to find him. Much less paperwork in a successful search than in recovering a dead body or, worse yet, a prolonged search with no conclusion.

The cabin was still slightly warm, though cooling fast with the door open to a wave of cool fresh air. There was no sign of the mysterious Kinka. The cabin was devoid of any clue he had been there.

"Where's the little guy?" Snow asked the troopers.

"What guy? No one here," Trooper Dick said.

"Well, who started the fire? How'd I get here?"

Snow seemed to be disoriented and talking nonsense.

"Get dressed. We're taking you home, Chief."

Aching and sore, especially in his leg and shoulder, Snow slipped on his Sam Browne belt with his holster, gun and radio, outer clothing, parka and boots. The troopers fired some questions at him that he did not answer. He pretended to be totally consumed with getting dressed, but his mind was buzzing. Instinctively he decided to be mum concerning Kinka and just give some basic facts about the crash and contact with the bear.

These two troopers were quite the pair. They were very smart, professional, and all around good cops. But they looked like Mutt and Jeff and could do a pretty good comedy shtick when they were so inclined, which they were clearly warming up to. Trooper Dick, as he was called, was a man of about six foot two. He had probably been quite a physical specimen when younger but had developed an impressively hard paunch. He was still a good-looking and imposing figure, with salt-and-pepper gray peeking out under his big round trooper hat, blue with a gold braid. He could retire whenever he felt the urge. He had at least twenty-five years, most of which was in the bush and could be measured like dog years. Alaskan years took a lot out of you. Trooper Debbie Roop was about a foot shorter and looked like a little sister.

Trooper Roop was no *cheechako* greenhorn either. She was a pilot and had done a couple years in the bush, though most of her time was in Anchorage or Fairbanks, the big cities. She had short, strawberry-blond hair, tendrils curling out from her own trooper hat, which looked much too big on her. She had freckles on her pert, upturned nose and at this moment looked much younger that her thirty-something years. Her parka hung almost to her knees. She was a "Mighty Mouse." Snow had seen her take down drunks twice her weight and cuff them.

"Could you give me a little light, Trooper Dick?" said Snow, not really a question—more of a polite way of saying "Move your fat ass out of the doorway." Trooper Dick could really fill up a doorway. He did almost as good a job of covering it as the door did.

Trooper Dick ignored the comment.

"How did you find me?" asked Snow.

"Easy. We found the plane and then followed your trail. It must have stopped snowing not long after you made it here. How did you find this place? I have never seen this before."

"That's hard to believe. I thought you knew every cabin and hunting shack in Bristol Bay," said Snow, which was true. Trooper Dick had flown or tromped all over the region.

"It was just dumb luck. I was trying to track Frank and Chubby but lost their trail after the deal with the bear. They must have gotten way ahead of me. We were hiking across the lake. I must have fallen twenty or thirty yards behind them. Snow was blowin' pretty stiff and I lost sight of them. Then I got in a scuffle with a grizzly. Damn near killed me, but I shot him. I made it to some scrub pines and the next thing I know I wound up here. Not much more to the story than that."

It was obvious to Snow that this was the first edition of the story they would be telling and retelling.

"How'd you know the plane went down?" Snow asked.

"Coasties got an ELT beacon last night," Trooper Dick said. "And you know the Coasties—can't find their asses with both hands. They called us to come check it out."

"You find Chubby and Frank N Beans?" Snow asked.

"Ya. We did a fly over in a Piper at first light. Saw them at a hunting cabin by the lake waving at us like crazy men. When we got to them they said you got lost in the storm."

Chief Snow got up slowly and Trooper Roop asked if he was hurt, which was good of her. Unlike her male partner, she was not afraid to show a human heart beating under the blue-and-gold state trooper uniform.

Snow elaborated about the bear attack and his wounds.

What the troopers told him was a bit of a shock.

"Your buddies weren't that far off. They saw the bear and took off running. When they thought it was safe, they went back looking for you. They said they heard shots, but by the time they got there you were gone. The snow covered your tracks," Trooper Dick said. "We expected to find you mauled to death on the lake."

"Well, you two picked up my trail. Doesn't sound like Chubby or Beans tried too hard."

"Remember, it was dark and blowy. It would have been hard to pick up your trail. They said they called for you. You hear anything?"

"Nope, just ringing in my ears from that damn bear smacking me around."

The chief wondered about that. Not that those guys would outright lie, but they most definitely would embellish things to ensure their good names, expanding their heroics over time. He could imagine them sweeping out a hundred feet or less and quickly returning to the cabin. "Nope, can't find him!"

Maybe it did not go like that, but Snow had a gut feeling they were not hunting for him with a brown bear on the loose, at night, and them with no gun. *Who could blame them?*

It was overcast—not snowing, but threatening. The temperature had warmed to just about zero. It felt downright balmy. Snow looked at the tracks as they walked away from the cabin. They had crossed the tracks from the night before. Snow asked the troopers how many sets they saw when they first found him. Trooper Dick stopped and looked at him.

"Two. Looks like you had company."

"Maybe. But I was out. I remember hearing a voice, but I don't remember a face," Snow said.

He quickly changed the subject, and they made their way to the troopers' plane parked on a small lake near Chubby's crash landing.

Chief Snow felt a sudden wave of emotion. He knew the state troopers were very good at what they did. They would have spared no effort or expense to find him or anyone who was lost. He felt unworthy and incompetent next to them, despite their humorous appearance. They were both smart and fearless.

"I appreciate you finding me. I can't tell you how grateful I am that it was you two searching. I would not trust anyone else to find me. I am your love slave for life."

Laughs all around by a relieved trio of bush blue-shirts. Trooper Roop gave the chief a sly look over her shoulder as she laughed. Snow was wondering if she was checking him out but then let that thought go away in a hurry.

As they approached the plane, Snow admired its paint job—a beautiful dark blue, with the Alaska state trooper seal on the tail and a yellow stripe leading from the seal halfway up the body of the plane. People in the village talked about the "blue plane" and how it affected them.

When the trooper plane flew in, it usually meant something big and bad had happened, like a death. There were stories about how guys who were in trouble or thought they *might* be in trouble headed for the hills to hide out when they saw the blue plane circling to land. The chief was never so happy to see a plane in his life.

Trooper Dick wanted to fly back to Dillingham, and he got his way of course. Snow just wanted to go home to the converted wood-stave water tank the city provided at no cost as his home. They called it "the Round House" because, well, it was round. The locals were not afraid to state the obvious.

Trooper Dick insisted that Snow get checked out at the real hospital in Dillingham, probably a good idea. Snow was pretty sure it was unnecessary but did not argue. Trooper Dick did not want to make a trip to Togiak and then back to his home base.

■ ■ ■

The little health clinic in Togiak did not have a doctor, only what they generously called nurses and a PA, a physician's assistant. In the village, you could die of many things that were routinely cured in the big city. That was one of the prices paid for living off the beaten track. People did not mind; they were used to it. Often, villagers planned vacations around trips to the doctor or dentist in Anchorage.

But the hub city of Dillingham had a real hospital. Chief Snow got a ride from Trooper Dick to Kanakanak Hospital. They chatted on the way. Trooper Dick did not have a very high opinion of Chubby—or Frank N Beans, for that matter. The pilot let his opinion be known in his faded blue Chevy Suburban with the trooper seal on the side. Chubby was disrespectful, and Beans was trouble, a hot head.

"Chubby was probably drunk and forgot to do his preflight checks. Maybe they had some bad gas or a fuel filter that needed looking at. He is a menace. Sure, he is—or *was*—a good pilot, but he is sloppier than Mattress Mary on Saturday night. You are lucky he didn't get y'all killed. Stupid drunk fuckhead."

Snow did not take the bait to comment on Chubby, though he was suitably impressed with the profanity-laced invective. Snow had a soft spot for the Irishman. He also still had a very high opinion of Chubby's ability as a pilot, despite his infatuation with the bottle.

Snow could never figure out big Dick. *How can someone live out here so long and look down his nose at everyone?* Snow could not understand it. It seemed to him that you had to develop a little tolerance out here, or you would go off the deep end. The troopers in general seemed to project that attitude, but Snow thought that inside Dick's uniform beat the heart of a normal man. There were some things you just could not get a grip on, it seemed.

"Hey you ever heard of a Native elder named Wasillie?" Snow asked Trooper Dick. Dick knew most folks by name, at least in this region.

Trooper Dick said, "There were Wasillies spread from Bethel to Port Moller. It was a pretty common name. I suppose there were a few that were recognized as elders."

Elder was a term of respect imparted by the community. Some folks were called elders even though they were not very old. In most villages, there was a group of elders to whom the community looked for guidance and who were placed on a pedestal. It was a part of the culture that was beautiful and natural. Chief Snow had met many elders and had always been impressed by how wise and humble each of them was. It was uncanny.

They pulled up to the Kanakanak hospital and Snow smiled as he thought of the hospital softball team's name. It had to be one of the all-time greatest names in the history of the world: the Kanakanak Kanakaknockers.

Before they got out, Snow casually asked Trooper Dick if he had ever heard of the Little People. Trooper Dick raised his eyebrows before he slid out and closed the door with enough force to rock the whole truck.

"Sure, I heard of the Little People. You're not *that* short, Snow," he laughed.

"Did you ever think there was anything to it?"

"Nah. Just an old wives' tale, or something made up by a drunken *siwash* with the DTs."

Snow had never heard Trooper Dick say the word *siwash* before, and it surprised him. *Siwash* meant drunken Native mix-breed, lazy good-for-nothing.

Trooper Dick was an enigma. He had done as much for the Natives as anyone, but here he was saying one of the worst words you could utter in reference to them. *Some things just don't make sense.* He thought that Dick was entitled an indiscretion now and again, but use of such an overt racial epithet troubled Snow.

"Why did ya ask about Little People, Chief? Did you see some out there when you were walking around delirious in the snow? Maybe one helped you find the cabin," Dick teased. *If he only knew,* thought Snow as he laughed it off.

■ ■ ■

Inside the hospital, Snow was quickly ushered into an exam room and given stellar treatment by the nurse. *Guess word has spread,* he thought. The nurse was a big-bosomed white woman with pale skin and red hair. Freckles sprinkled her nose like cinnamon sugar on toast. She was from somewhere in the lower forty-eight, but Snow could not remember where. The nurse talked a lot.

"So, rumor has it you got into a tussle with a bear. That true?" the nurse asked. When Snow did not immediately answer, the nurse filled the void. "Did you get mauled or bitten? Any scratches or anything? What'd you go and tangle with a bear for anyway?" The nurse peppered the police chief like she was shooting scattershot at a duck.

She was nice enough, but Snow was less comfortable with the direct ways of white folks than the more subtle, less intrusive demeanor of the Natives. A Native would not have even brought up the bear attack. Snow made a bit of small talk, preferring to ask her how things were going rather than answering questions about what happened. That was Snow's manner anyway, not just today.

When Snow uncovered his injuries, she looked surprised. She apparently did not really expect to see claw and bite marks on his body. Chief Snow looked with interest at the marks as well; he was not used to seeing them.

The redhead recovered quickly.

"Why did the bear attack you?" she asked. Again she did not give Snow time to answer, but he was not really inclined to answer her silly questions.

"Were you carrying food, or in its territory? This is their country, you know. You don't want to needlessly attract them or do things to irritate the bears. I thought all you cops got trained in that stuff?"

Snow did not respond to the nurse's comments. Instead he asked, "Do bites or scratches like these get infected easily?"

"I am sure they can, just like any other bite, like from a dog or something," she responded. Her body language suggested that she didn't really know what she was talking about. She quickly left as though his question was somehow an affront.

After some time, Dr. Perez stopped by. He was the primary physician for this region and was based in Dillingham. He was a kind, wonderful man of about forty-five. He came from Mexico but had lived in remote Alaska for many years. As he often did, Snow wondered at how people from such far corners of the world ended up in the middle of nowhere in Alaska.

Dr. Perez was balding with black hair. His eyes had an amused twinkle most of the time. He had a confident manner and trustworthy hands.

After Dr. Perez looked him over, he told Snow that the wounds looked very clean and good. Whatever Kinka had used as a balm had dried and mostly brushed off. What was left looked like dirt or lint. The doctor said they usually got red and infected quickly if not treated. He asked if Snow had treated them. Snow sometimes hated doctors because they were like cops and had built-in lie detectors. Snow could tell that Dr. Perez had just flicked on his bullshit monitor.

Snow offered what he thought was a clever response. "The only thing I did was wash them out, Doc."

Dr. Perez gave him a wry smile. "Well, then you must have good resistance to infection."

Dr. Perez was clever. Snow just agreed and let it go. Dr. Perez directed the nurse to wash and disinfect Snow's wounds and prescribed some antibiotics and pain medication. After a few final comments on how often to change the dressing, Dr. Perez left.

A short, attractive brown-skinned woman came in the examination room to assist the bigger, brassier nurse. The smaller nurse got the chief's attention without trying. The red-headed nurse left the room, which left the little attractive nurse to tend to the chief's wounds.

Snow instantly looked for a wedding ring, an unusual thing for him to do. The nurse had not spoken a word, which intrigued him and also warmed his blood, as they both seemed focused on her hands feeling his body. She seemed demure but also quietly confident.

"I don't think we have met. I'm Chief Snow of Togiak. What is your name?"

She did not immediately answer. Chief Snow thought at first that she was Native but thought she could be Asian, too. When she spoke, he was sure she was not local.

"I am Lilly. Are you married?"

Snow's eyebrows shot up. She was certainly not afraid to speak her mind.

"Well, no. I'm single," Snow stammered

"Me too. I'm from Anchorage but lived with family in Dillingham."

She was the most beautiful woman Snow had ever seen. His pulse raced and he flushed. *Geez, like a frigging teenager,* he thought.

"You sure you are not married?" she asked, showing an apparent lack of trust for all things male. He could only nod. She was direct in a way that did not offend.

Chief Snow recovered some but was knocked off balance by her manner and gentle touch. Her immaculate straight black hair hung down to her small, shapely behind, which was well defined under her blue scrubs. Her skin was a golden brown, and her dark brown, pecan-shaped eyes sparkled when she looked at him. Her face was an almost perfect heart shape. She had beautiful white teeth and full lips. She was fine boned, with fine black hair on her slender arms. Her wrists were almost impossibly dainty. She looked like she was very young, but he guessed she was older than she looked. He was strangely aroused by the dark hair on her arms.

She finished her work before Snow was ready for her to leave. Snow had to know her full name, and he asked her.

"Lilly Wasillie," she said. Just like that, she was gone, but she gave him a little peek as she turned the corner.

Snow got his instructions, some pain pills, and antibiotics and left the hospital. He immediately regretted that he had not gotten Lilly's phone number—or at least asked for it. *I am a cop,* he thought with encouragement. *I deal in information.* He was determined to get her number and call her.

Snow wondered about Lilly Wasillie. Her sheer beauty made an impact on him. *Does she have a boyfriend? Could she be related to the ancient Elder Wasillie who met Captain Shoemaker, according to the mysterious Kinka?*

CHAPTER 4
THE VILLAGE

Charlie Johnson was a Togiak Native of mixed blood. He was also a direct descendant of a bull cook for the whaling vessel *Saint George*, captained by Sir Jonathan Shoemaker. The small English ship was north hunting whales for their oil a little too late in the fall of 1871. Ice trapped it there. Crewmen went ashore to make contact with the Native people and hunt, as their provisions were very low.

This was the first contact by the Native people of Togiak with outside people besides the other tribes in the region. Captain Shoemaker and his strange-looking crewmen were welcomed into the village. All the people were fascinated by the men from the boat, who were not all Englishmen. A variety of races and countries were represented.

The huts were constructed of whalebones, dug into the ground, and roofed with chunks of tundra. At least half of each small home was underground. Some of the bigger homes had several rooms in which residents could actually stand. The floors were covered with furs of "parka" squirrels, caribou, and even polar bears. Strings of dried fish hung from the roof joists. A fire pit in the center of the main room was used for cooking and heat. Much of the food was dried or boiled.

Captain Shoemaker and his men spent considerable time ashore. Some of the crew was left aboard to ensure the safety of the *Saint George*, but the others spent time with the Natives of Togiak. Bull cook Isaac Johnson from Ireland was one of the men ashore with Captain Shoemaker.

Johnson was short and stout with red hair and a swarthy complexion burnt by the salt spray and sun. He was spry and easy to like. He smiled often, which revealed a set of rotted and broken teeth—those he had left at thirty-two years. But he had a good smile nonetheless and soon he caught the eye of a Native maiden by the name of Puniq. She was fourteen and just of age. Isaac and Puniq were soon sleeping together under the wolf furs, and they were happy with each other.

Others in the crew also found mates among the local Yupik Eskimo and even began to speak the language. The winters started early and lasted long in that part of the world. When the ice began to break up in May, several of the crew asked Captain Shoemaker to stay behind, to which he agreed. One of those men was Isaac Johnson; Puniq was with child.

The following summer, the elders requested that the outsiders build their own huts away from the main village. There were some problems that could best be resolved by having the newcomers and their mates move a short distance away. The new cluster of huts became known as Jabbertown for the odd and varied languages the men spoke.

■ ■ ■

Charlie Johnson did not know of his heritage or relation to Isaac Johnson of Ireland or much about Captain Shoemaker's whaling vessel, the *Saint George*. He did know about Jabbertown, though, and that is exactly where he had hidden his stash of illegal alcohol. He smuggled in two cases of Popov vodka from Dillingham. Charlie endured fourteen hours of rough snow-machining on his Ski-Doo each way to bring back the precious cargo. He did not drink anything on the way back, a challenge he was glad for. It made him push harder to get back!

Charlie was twenty-nine. He was sure he had some white blood but did not know the full extent of his Anglo DNA. His facial features and complexion were northern European. He was an attractive man with a handsome smile. His eyes and lower body hinted of his Yupik heritage. In Charlie's mind, he was Native first. He was ashamed of his white blood because it marked him as a half-breed: part *gussok*. Charlie was only about five foot nine, with a medium build and a pretty well-developed upper body from pulling nets in the summer. What frightened people about Charlie was not his size or his strength. Charlie Johnson was wild, unpredictable, and downright scary crazy at times.

Charlie only brought five bottles of alcohol with him into town; the rest he stashed under a beached, derelict, gray wooden skiff near the whalebone remnants of Jabbertown. He slid the remaining twenty-seven bottles of alcohol into two boxes under the wreck's exposed corner. The rest was covered with snow. It was a good hiding place for now, and he was careful to cover his tracks. He would probably have to move the alcohol if he did not sell it all right away. Once folks found out you had alcohol, they would hound you mercilessly until you were out. If they suspected you had a cache somewhere, people would follow you to the ends of the earth or track you to try and spot where you had hidden the cache. Charlie knew because he had been successful at it himself.

Charlie paid about $180 for the cheap vodka, not counting

the gas for his Ski-Doo. Well, technically the gas was stolen or borrowed, and the Ski-Doo was a loaner—without the owner's technical consent, though his uncle would be happy enough with a jug or two as payment. He would make the money back by selling two bottles; the going rate was $200 a pint depending on availability. It was hard to come by lately. That son of a bitch Chief Snow had been clamping down.

Charlie smiled. He actually liked Chief Snow. *Decent guy for a cop.* They had some history together and Snow was not half bad for a gussok. At least, Charlie thought he was a gussok. Some people said he was part Native. *Who knows and who cares?* thought Charlie. He had stashed the jugs of booze, and it was time to slide into town.

He went all the way to Dillingham on the booze run because it was impossible to get caught. Or almost impossible. You had to be a moron to get caught, and Chief Snow caught more than one of the village morons sledding back with a load of booze this winter. It was even riskier coming in with it on a plane or mailing it in. The shit was heavy, which the postal workers and baggage handlers could catch.

Charlie was careful as he came into town on a lesser-used trail with a good view of the village. He did not know that Chief Snow had not been in town, or about the crash-landing or Snow getting swatted by a bear. What he did know was that he was anxious to get drunk and then laid. Johnson had passed within a couple miles of where Chief Snow shot the bear. It was hard work riding the snow machine over rough terrain for that many hours. It was loud and cold. He had been focused on getting back.

Togiak was beginning to get some light as spring approached. It was light about six hours a day now. In the dead of winter, if there was no cloud cover, Togiak got an hour or two of light midday. Winters were very long near the Arctic Circle. It got worse as you went north. Barrow suffered two months of total darkness. At least in Togiak they got *some* light. It was a little warmer there, too.

In the summer the sun never got tired. It was always light, it seemed. Everyone's energy picked up, too, and it was common to see kids out playing or riding four-wheelers at midnight in the surreal twilight. Folks worked on their boats at all hours of the night or went off to the hunting camps accessible by skiff or four-wheeler up the coast. You could drive the beach for about twenty miles in a truck. Occasionally a truck would break down. Once in a great while, a vehicle would get swamped by the tide, which rushed in. If you let the air out of your tires down to about ten pounds, you could get through the sand pretty good—one of the tricks the locals had learned.

Snow got into town a couple hours before Johnson. While he worked his way back to Togiak, Chubby, Skinny, and their crew were busy with the Cessna stuck on the lake. They got it running fairly quickly; the fuel pump was the problem. Chubby had thought as much and so brought a new one, along with a spare propeller, which he and Skinny quickly replaced.

On their return to Dillingham, Skinny flew low and spotted a dead brown bear. He radioed Chubby and they both flew over to get a good look. Chubby confirmed it was the same bear that they had buzzed and that later attacked the chief.

Chubby spread word quickly that Snow had shot and killed a grizzly with his pistol. The news beat the chief back to Togiak. When he got off the plane, Bill Tuzzy was there to greet him, flashing his gap-toothed smile as he explained how he got the news over the VHF. Tuzzy was the airline agent for three of the four local air carriers. The only one he did not represent was King Air, which only came three times a week at most. He threw Snow a bone and let him be the agent for King Air.

Being an agent for the local carriers was hard work. Tuzzy worked the phone all the time, talking to people who wanted to book flights to Dillingham and then talking to his counterpart on the other end. Flights were coming and going all the time. Tuzzy kept a little notebook in his pocket to write down the names of those who called. Freight just got tossed on as it came in, so you never knew for sure when your stuff was getting to town. Tuzzy would simply drop off freight at people's houses.

King Air did much less traffic but received a lucrative mail contract, so that was the basis of their trips to Togiak three times a week. Snow accompanied the plane and hauled the mail back to drop off at the village post office. He had to handle passengers too, but it was not that much work. One fringe benefit: Snow could catch rides to Dillingham for free.

A substantial part of his job as police chief dealt with trying to stem the flow of bootleg alcohol to the village. That meant meeting as many planes as he could to see who was coming and going. He worked with the carriers and made a serious dent in the alcohol coming in. But it was an impossible task. Despite his efforts, a good share of illegal booze still made it through. There were just too many planes and boxes of freight constantly coming and going.

Tuzzy was six feet tall and skinny. His face was ruddy from working in the frigid air, loading and off-loading the twenty to thirty planes that came and left in a typical week. Tuzzy was an interesting man. His house was a conglomeration of plywood, metal Conex containers and the fuselage of a DC-4 that had crashed on approach to Togiak years ago. It was too expensive to fly the plane out for repair, so Tuzzy salvaged the remains. He dragged it into town and attached it to his house. Tuzzy was a self-taught carpenter—forever learning, it seemed. Nothing went to waste in this part of the bush.

Tuzzy came to the bush years ago to work a construction job for a few months. He was still there trying to get rich twenty years later. Chief Snow was of the opinion that Tuzzy was no longer suited to the real world. That happened to people. Tuzzy was now permanently half a bubble off level, but he was decent folk and the hardest worker in Togiak. He also knew everyone and everything that came and went. Snow knew that Tuzzy knew everyone who was bringing in alcohol and that Tuzzy would never snitch. Tuzzy had determined long ago that ignorance, or at least a tight lip, was key to his survival.

Chief Snow gingerly stepped down the skinny, swaying gangway of the Piper Cherokee. He was the only passenger; the rest was freight and mail. He was sore and glad he had gotten some painkillers from Doc Perez. Tuzzy clapped Snow on the back and the chief winced.

"That brown bar you shot died, Chief! You got a license for shooting bar? Haw haw!"

"I was lucky to get away. That was a mean one. Knocked me around like a garbage can. The bear shoulda had the license to hunt me," the chief smiled. "I wasn't even sure I hit it."

Something in his gut told him that Kinka of the Little People had told him the truth about the bear.

"They say you got mauled up some, Chief. That little brownie was going to eat you for an hors-devours. Haw. I guess he died of lead poisoning!"

News was scarce out here, and it traveled fast whether good or bad. Chief Snow might have to endure a little celebrity for a while, which he did not look forward to. He really liked Tuzzy, though, and favored him with a few details of the crash and the ordeal with the bear. Tuzzy listened attentively. He knew he was getting valuable horse's-mouth information. Such information was like hard currency—even better than that—out here on the edge of the world; just being the bearer of news could bring a certain measure of notoriety. He cautiously asked a question, not wanting to push the chief, who only ever grudgingly shared information. The only reason the chief was sharing was because the bear attack only involved him. He'd never discuss a case.

Tuzzy quickly unloaded the freight and bypass mail as Snow sat in the cab of the truck. Tuzzy gave him a ride to town, but the Chief was done talking about the ordeal. Instead he asked Tuzzy about what was going on. Tuzzy was happy and jabbered about some trivial things as he negotiated the truck over the two snow-packed miles into Togiak. He did not give up information easily either.

Togiak's name meant a "place for sending" in Yupik because Togiak was a hub for sending supplies to the even smaller villages deeper into the bush. Togiak was a traditional Yupik village where most people hunted and fished for subsistence. A kind of hybrid Yupik language was spoken, but there was no written language until around 1950 when missionaries helped the people develop one.

The village had a population of about 900 and sat on the western edge of Bristol Bay. The region was renowned for its fishing, in particular the summer salmon runs, some of the largest in the world. But people also fished herring in the spring or simply gathered herring eggs and kelp by hand when the tide was out. Herring eggs, or "spawn on kelp," was something of a local delicacy.

Snow liked salmon, which was plentiful in the summer. The herring eggs or spawn were eaten raw. In an interesting cultural blend, many people put soy sauce on them. Snow had eaten plenty herring eggs at gatherings but really could take it or leave it. The roe simply tasted like salt water.

The village stretched north to south on the beach but was being gradually threatened by the tides. Around 1975, the townspeople moved the infrastructure of the village several miles to save it from the encroaching sea. Most of the town was still by the water, but eventually, as the buildings got old and worn out, the townspeople would build in the new site.

■ ■ ■

Snow watched the cemetery roll by. It was surrounded by a whalebone fence that arched as high as ten feet in an impressive array of fossils. On the right was the "Million Dollar Hill," as the locals called the great gravel pile. It overlooked "Hepatitis Lake" where all the "honey buckets" got dumped. One good thing about year-round cold weather was that it froze all the waste, limiting the smell.

They snaked through the village, which paralleled the beach, some houses mere feet from the seawall. Some 900 people or so lived there, and all but a few were Native Alaskans. Most of the houses lacked paint and were as gray and dingy as an old dishrag. Those that had paint were brightly colored. Oddly, many were partially painted, as if whoever was doing the job went inside for something or got tired and never came back. More likely, they simply ran out of paint and there was no more to be had in the village. A couple houses painted a variety of colors gave evidence to that theory.

They drove by the police station. The small building had banana-yellow metal siding and doubled as the fire station, housing the one ancient fire truck. Snow decided against stopping; he was drained. If there was an emergency, everyone knew to find him at the Round House.

The house was an old 30,000-gallon water tank about thirty feet in diameter. It had been painted red some years ago but was now as gray as the sky above. Snow thanked Tuzzy and slid out of the truck onto the frozen ground. Tuzzy just barely came to a stop to let Snow out and was gone. Tuzzy was a busy man with freight to unload.

The Round House was owned by the village of Togiak, and Chief Snow lived upstairs, where there was a kitchen, bedroom and bath. Downstairs housed a laundry room right inside the entry, a couple more bedrooms, and a bathroom. The village used the spare rooms to house itinerant or traveling nurses, dentists, or basically anyone who came into the village to work as a traveler. In fact, a physician's assistant, or PA, had recently been staying there. Most of the time Snow had the place to himself, but the house was public property, and the main door was never locked.

Snow stood outside and had a smoke as he looked out over Togiak Bay. Off to his left a mile or so was the mouth of the Togiak River. Everything was frozen for now. He thought for about the thousandth time that they could have been more imaginative when they named things around here.

On the other side of the Round House was a small creek named Two Sisters in memory of twin sisters who drowned in the creek in 1971. *Imaginative*, thought Snow, *though kind of morbid.*

Snow entered his circular, formerly aquatic abode. He was surprised to find Stanley Beans, Frank N Beans's brother, in the laundry room entrance. Stanley did not turn around; he was busy putting clothing into the dryer. The tall, mentally handicapped man named Smally was also in attendance. He seemed to just pop up here and there, usually someplace he thought he might get coffee or smoke.

"Coffee! Smoke!" Smally directed at Snow, holding out the greasy glass pint jar he drank coffee from.

"No coffee, Smally," said the chief as he fished out a couple smokes and handed them over. Smally went outside without a word, eager to smoke.

"Hey, Stanley. Washing my laundry?"

"Eee! My laundry, Chief."

"You can do your laundry here, Stanley. Just appreciate if you let me know first so I don't accidentally shoot you."

Snow could not be too peeved at Stanley, even though he was sneaking in to do his laundry. Many folks did not have washing machines or dryers. A lot of people didn't even have flush toilets in their houses. "Honey bucket" was the euphemism for the device people used to do their private business. It came from the refrain "Honey, take out the bucket."

Stanley Beans was mostly skin and bones. He wore very thick lens in black-framed glasses, which tended to make him appear bug-eyed. He had a couple front teeth missing, but that did not deter him from showing them all the time; he was always either smiling or grimacing. It was often hard to tell which. Stanley was a likable fellow like his older brother, Frank, but with a better vocabulary. He was only about five foot five. His face was gaunt. His high cheekbones stood out in the dark-brown, pocked skin of his face.

Stanley often served as Snow's jail guard when he had a prisoner. It was certainly not a full-time job, but Stanley was around enough to bond with the chief. They often ate lunch together or shared stories, and the chief had offered Stanley the use of his washer and dryer.

Snow entered the main house and slowly climbed the metal spiral staircase to the second floor. He looked around his home. The main room was nearly a perfect circle, the only flaw in the arc a small bedroom set off of one wall. It was a huge, spacious room with a million angles. The ceiling peaked in the middle, a good fourteen feet above his head, where the original wood used to build the water tank was visible.

Off to the left was the kitchen and in the center the TV, which picked up the one available channel. On the entire wall facing the water was a series of windows that rose eight feet from the floor, making for a panoramic view of the beach. A door opened onto a small, rickety deck. The deck was not good for much other than going out for a smoke.

Snow was struck by a wave of melancholy. Maybe it was the sudden mortality check caused by the plane and the grizzly. He thought about the woman, the nurse Lilly. She seemed to be in his head all the time now. She caused him to realize how lonely he was. Such feelings were usually under tight wraps. He went to bed thinking of her.

CHAPTER 5
THE JOB

C hief Snow showed up at the office around ten. It had been almost three weeks since the plane crash, his tussle with the grizzly, and the encounter—real or imagined—with Kinka of the Little People.

Despite his angst, the chief felt some relief because it looked like "break up" had finally arrived. "Spring break up," or just "break up," was a term Alaska adopted from the oil industry. It was when spring finally hit and the frost came out of the ground, making the gravel roads soft and muddy. Coupled with the runoff from the snow melt, the roads could get downright impassable.

In Togiak the roads were a real mess—deep, life-threatening ruts, and potholes filled with water runoff. People had been rumored to disappear in some of the bigger ones. *We need to get the grader working to smooth things out,* thought Snow. The chief looked around the office and headed for the beat-up coffee maker to start a pot. "Police station and fire hall" was a pretty generous way of describing the small building. There was a big open room with a refrigerator, coffeepot and such adjacent to the small office the chief used as his own. Past the office were a couple small jail cells and a hallway to the bathroom, which was complete with a flush toilet hooked to a tank that had to be pumped out when full. It was a luxury to have a flush toilet of any kind.

Beyond the bathroom was the garage. An old fire truck sat back there waiting patiently for the next house fire it would attend. It was not good for much. If the tired truck started at all, that was a good thing. It was handy for at least attempting to make sure the houses next to the one on fire were watered down.

A lot of people had woodstoves for burning driftwood scavenged from the beach. Some had small oil-burning stoves. Because it got so cold, the stoves were always in use and often burned really hot. House fires were an unfortunate consequence of living in the bush. Someday the whole town would probably go up in smoke.

The floor in the kitchen, which doubled as a main office, had off-white tile that ended abruptly and turned into plywood worn with visible footpaths. There was that same sense of incompletion as the half-painted houses. Someone had started the job with good intentions, only to run out of floor tiles. Ten years later, the floor still needed another couple boxes of tile, which it would probably never get.

There was an old metal desk used by Stanley Beans, emergency jail guard and real-life, Native version of Barney Fife, except that Chief Snow did not even give him one bullet.

No one had been jailed since the last rash of bootleg whiskey made the rounds a week ago. Sometimes the locals made decent homebrew, and once Snow had even busted an ambitious sort who had made a small still. By and large the homebrew was nasty stuff—a rancid concoction of orange juice, yeast, and sugar. Sometimes folks could not wait until the yeast was done doing its thing and would dip into the stew with bottles or cups. Several such unfortunates ended up in the clinic vomiting because they lacked patience for the necessary aging of a day or so.

At least it was better than drinking Lysol or Listerine, Snow thought. *Alcoholics Anonymous wouldn't stand a chance here.*

Snow remembered a sexual assault case from last summer at the cannery. Jig Johnson had grabbed a store clerk, pulled her in the back storeroom, and groped her while he tried to lick her tonsils. Jig was just a little too juiced on mouthwash to understand that *no* means *no.* Because there were no police over at the cannery to slow down ole Jig, he just got in his skiff and left after the nubile clerk extricated herself from his slobbery embrace. Jig fled across the river to Togiak, somehow avoiding drowning.

The molested clerk told her boss, who told the super, who called Snow across the river to report the attempted rape. Had the young and pretty clerk from the lower forty-eight had more exposure to the drunken destitution of the bush, she probably would have just beaned Jig with a can of baked beans or something.

Women took a beating in the bush, which was the hard truth. Most who grew up there had been raped at some time in their lives—only once if they were lucky. Often it was a relative or someone close. Some women absorbed the torment; others, like the clerk and even Mattress Mary in town, complained, sued or fought back. The chief investigated a couple cases of a girlfriend or wife blowing off their guy's head. The women typically avoided jail because they acted in self-defense.

Such violence seemed out of character for the otherwise subdued, respectful local Natives. But when the Natives drank they became different. Rape, murder, assault, and suicide were good prospects when enough alcohol was in town. The alcohol seemed to be the catalyst for violence and was almost always involved. It was a curse and had ruined or damaged many lives.

When Chief Snow had received the call about the assault, he

knew where Jig would be headed, which was across the river and back to his home in town. The chief went to a lookout spot with a good view of the river. He used the field glasses and watched Jig's perilous escape from the cannery. The tide was out, and Jig pulled his skiff right up into a god-awful patch of slimy stinky mud. Jig had already stumbled to the bow, falling hard once, and tossed the anchor onto the beach. Jig sobered suddenly when he saw Snow approach. His alcohol-soaked brain decided to make a run for it. He started the kicker and began to back away from the beach.

Snow waded into the muck in a futile attempt to stop Jig's retreat, but the anchor did its job; it dug in as Jig backed away. When the line went taut, it was a pure miracle Jig did not sail over the kicker. He was so drunk that he did not seem to understand *why* he could not get away. He traced crescent-moon patterns back and forth at full throttle. He was too pickled to figure out he just needed to make some slack off the anchor line. Jig killed the motor as the prop dug in the mud. Snow, smirking and shaking his head, called to Jig.

"Hey, Jig! Come in here before you kill yerself!"

Jig looked at Snow like he'd seen him for the first time. He moved forward and tripped, falling facedown in the skiff. *That's gonna hurt tomorrow,* thought Snow, who had waded forward in the slime to the anchor line. He pulled the fourteen-foot red Lund into shore. Jig's face appeared above the bow.

"Jeez, Jig, let me give you a hand. You are cooked!" said Snow, using the Togiak word for highly intoxicated.

Jig smiled and began to swing over the edge of the boat. What followed was a failed experiment. A man whose feet were sunken in mud tried to prevent a plastered man from tumbling ass over teakettle off the bow. A resounding *Splat!* resonated on the calm, gray water. Snow interfered with Jig's swan dive, messing up an otherwise perfect ten, as onlookers on the beach laughed and applauded. Live entertainment! Snow landed on top of Jig and desperately tried to prevent the ruination of his clothing.

Trying to extract himself, Snow lost his right boot, which was sucked off by the tidal mud. He used Jig for balance as he attempted to reinsert his foot into his shoe. In slow motion, they danced the mud dance, with a slow pirouette followed by a graceful full facial into the poop.

Snow spit and muttered a few choice epithets. They were both black from head to toe and slimed with the smell of rotten fish. Snow abandoned Jig and let him flail and blubber while he wiggled his shoe loose from the fierce mud. He was going to put it on but said "Fuck it" and pulled off his other boot. He tied the laces together and hung them around his neck. Jig had moved about a foot forward during this time.

Jail will feel good after this, Jig, the chief thought.

Gathering onlookers giggled behind their hands at the show, trying not to disrespect the man charged with protecting them. Snow pretended not to notice. Any outrage from him would only make the story better and live longer.

Snow helped Jig up and they slithered the final twenty feet, until safely on the wet, hard black sand. What a muddy sight they made walking arm and arm past the seawall to the chief's truck.

"Where are we going?" Jig slurred.

"To get cleaned up," Snow said. "Get in the bed, and if ya try jumping out, I'll shoot you." Jig's eyebrows went up at that.

At the station they stripped down and hosed off in icy water from the hose in the garage. Snow gave Jig a towel.

"You been drinking Lysol, Jig? I smell like a damn dentist office."

Jig admitted sheepishly that he had indeed been drinking alcohol. Before Snow got around to eliciting a confession from Jig for groping the clerk, Jig stood boldly and said, "She wanted me bad, Chief."

Snow had an enlightening Q and A with Jig about the relative merits of Lysol as compared to, say, Scope or some other over-the-counter medicines or cleaning supplies people would drink for the alcohol in them. Jig even shared the various methods of consumption.

"Well, some folks says you should strain it through bread, or even a sock. I just drink it straight from the bottle or can. No point in fooking around."

Snow belched a pathetic laugh, but Jig's crime was not funny—violence and attempted rape. He led Jig into the jail cell and dialed the area magistrate.

■ ■ ■

Snow got a can of Eagle Claw sweetened condensed milk from the fridge and lightened his coffee to his liking. Smally came into the office holding a filthy pint jar.

"Coffee?!"

"Sure, Smally. Let me clean your cup first."

Snow patiently washed Smally's old fruit jar and rinsed it before pouring it about half full of coffee. Then he filled the jar near to the top with lukewarm water. He had learned to either give him decaf or water his coffee down; caffeine made Smally a real pest.

"Smoke?!"

Snow pulled out a couple Winston Lights and gave them to Smally, who also asked for "Light?!"

"That is all for now. Don't come back until later," Snow said. "Do you want me to stick around and put it out for you, too?" The joke was lost on Smally, who already on his way out the door, anxious to smoke.

Smally was maybe forty; hard to say. He was tall and not a bad-looking man. He wore a crumpled black felt hat and walked with a stiff-legged gait. He had been a normal man once but was clubbed over the head in a drunken brawl and was never the same—or so the story went. Smally was a Vietnam vet and a Native born in Togiak who now lived in a twelve-by-twelve shack behind his parents' house. He lived for coffee and cigarettes and bummed them where he could. The chief was among his easiest marks.

Smally scared the bejeesus out of Snow on Snow's first night in town, coming into the Round House in the middle of the night saying "Smoke?" and startling Snow out of bed. After he got his heart back into his chest, he figured out that Smally was, well, not right. He had a soft spot for Smally.

■ ■ ■

The phone rang and Snow received a complaint that Peter Nanilchik's dogs were howling again. According to the caller, Peter was not feeding them.

Snow went out into the sun. It was a heat wave today, up in the forties. He brought his coffee with him. He had a nice new plastic cup with a lid on it. He was pretty proud of the cup, which he put into the stained and dusty cup holder in the battered, white Isuzu Trooper. The coffee stains all over the dash were evidence of failed attempts at bringing coffee with him in the past, but that was before the neat new insulated coffee mug.

As he drove toward Pete's house, Snow pondered the awful condition of the road, full of holes but dusty as well. *Surely God is punishing us for some transgressions,* he thought. A four-wheeler came flying around the gentle curve and Snow drove straight through a series of bone-jarring potholes he had intended to drive around. The new coffee mug flew out of its holder and exploded off the windshield, showering coffee inside the cab.

Snow was so aggravated that he ignored the whole mess and kept driving. *If I don't acknowledge it, then it did not happen.* He pulled in front of Pete's house on the edge of town. A cloud of dust rolled over the truck as Snow got out.

"You need to get one of those new coffee cups with a lid, Chief. Then you won't get so much on you," Pete said with a grin.

Chief Snow politely ignored the advice.

"What's the deal with the dogs, Pete?"

"Well, I just don't have the time to work them, to run them like I want to."

Snow went back to check on the dogs, which were a sorry sight. *It would be a blessing for these dogs to get a new home,* he thought. There were eleven of them, all dying of starvation and mangy as hell. A few folks in town kept sled dogs. It was kind of a throwback to the times when people used them to get around. But no one actually used them for transportation anymore; they were raised for fun or sled dog races like the Iditarod. People would have the dogs pull a four-wheeler instead of a sled for training. The dogs were tied up to stakes in the ground; some had small houses. Unfortunately, the dogs were sometimes neglected.

"These guys look in bad shape, Pete. What do you say I take them off your hands?"

Pete pondered for a minute, stroking his chin. "Probably for the best, Chief."

Snow worked quickly and loaded up six of the starving, pathetic animals in his truck. He wished he could do something else with the dogs, but he knew what he had to do—shoot them one by one in the head. There was no one to take the dogs and no animal control officer. Essentially, the job of animal control fell to the chief.

He disposed of the dogs at the city dump and came back for the last five. He told Peter no more dogs unless Peter checked with him first. Then he took care of the rest.

The dogs smelled really bad and had never been cleaned. They lived on salmon scraps, which made them reek. Each dog had lived at the end of a six-foot chain. Snow guessed that they were some remnant of the past for Pete.

■ ■ ■

Snow returned to the office and hosed down the bed of his truck, ripe with vomit and feces. Afterward he drove out of town into the foothills. He needed some time after that bad duty. He got to the end of the road, which overlooked the town and had a view into a valley.

What Snow saw surprised and awed him. Off in the distance about a mile or so, he saw hundreds of caribou grazing. He wondered why no one had told him the caribou were close. Maybe they snuck in and no one knew it. It was an impressive sight. He wondered if the main herd was out of sight on the other side of the hills.

He stood there and watched the caribou cavort and graze while he smoked to clear his head. He thought about Nurse Lilly again. He had only seen her once since he met her at the hospital.

It was after Frank N Beans had sobered up and was released from jail. Frank had done very well staying sober since rampaging around the town that night. He checked in every day at the police department for a breathalyzer test, which was a condition of his release. Snow did not make Beans suffer the indignity of blowing into the breathalyzer. He could tell from a hundred feet away whether Beans had been drinking. Usually, the two had a cup of coffee and a smoke unless one of them was in a hurry to get somewhere, which was seldom the case.

Judge Sadie rewarded Beans by suspending most of his jail time. Beans had not contested the charges, which was probably smart. The DA was a fire-breather and Snow had a good case against Beans.

Judge Sadie tended to respect those who admitted their wrongs and sentenced people commensurately. She made him spend a couple days in jail to remind him of the serious nature of his wrongs and to give him a look at his future home if he did not behave. Beans opted to do his time before fishing season got underway and turned himself in to Snow, who was obligated to take him to Dillingham.

Actually, Snow did a little finagling. He had been looking to get over to Dillingham. So he pulled a couple strings and lined things up to take Beans to do his time. He did a little basic police work and got Lilly's number as well as gossip about her. But there wasn't much to gather. She was half Native and half other stuff, mostly Filipino and white. She lived with her cousins and grandfather, or *appa*, in Dillingham. She was from up north but had come here from Anchorage where she attended nursing school. She had not been in town that long and mostly worked, keeping to herself. She did not have a boyfriend that anyone knew of.

Snow called Lilly and they agreed to meet at the hospital.

When they met the second time, there was some awkward tension. Snow expected to waltz into town and immediately win her affection. He thought about her constantly, and in his imagined narrative she had been doing the same thing. He felt a connection when they met—he was sure of it.

But Lilly had other ideas. She knew men out here. They were brusque and could be coarse. She had no intention of getting involved with a ruffian, though Snow certainly seemed sensitive and kind, at least on the surface. She was going to do what women have been doing since time began: make the man twist in the wind. She wanted to take her time, and that was exactly the way it was going to be.

Snow asked her to dinner, and they went, but not before she brought him to meet her cousins and grandfather. She wanted to watch him in the company of others. Her heart fluttered for this man she barely knew. She told herself to calm down and not get her hopes up.

Lilly had also done a bit of basic research on Snow. She knew he was single and had been working in Togiak as police chief for a couple years or so. He had a good reputation. There was no apparent woman in his life, and it appeared he hadn't dated anyone in his time in Togiak.

She wondered about that. It could mean he was discerning and didn't want to get involved with a local woman because of his job. It could also mean he was a weirdo or that he was closet gay. Lilly was nothing if not realistic and practical. Her hopes had been dashed in the past. When it came to men in Alaska, "the odds are good, but the goods are odd."

The house was a nice-looking A-frame surrounded by scrub spruce trees. There was a thirty-two-foot aluminum gill-net boat at the side of the house. The boat was up on blocks with fifty-five gallon drums on either side to balance it. There was a metal shed next to the boat. Inside, Snow saw a stout man sitting at a bench hanging gear for the upcoming fishing season. The man stared at Snow but did not get up. Snow was impressed at the apparent affluence of Lilly's cousins. Snow thought they must be good fishermen and probably refrained from alcohol.

Lilly led Snow into the house. She walked him through the spacious kitchen and introduced him to her grandfather, who was sitting by the fire, carving a piece of ivory. He set the ivory and tool on an end table.

"Chief Snow, Appa Niki Wasillie," Lilly said in her sparse way. She was still wearing scrubs from work. She went to change clothes and left him there alone with Grandpa Niki. As she left, she melted Snow with a smile. Lilly then smiled to herself. She knew she was putting Snow through some paces with her family. But she was determined not to give her heart to someone unworthy. She needed someone strong, a man of character.

When she first told her family about Snow's visit, two of her cousins took umbrage.

"No gussok cops in my house," said Cousin Tukok, with menace.

"Eee!" Cousin Pukok agreed.

The two cousins were both powerful and large. They looked fat but were in fact just big. They had the unkempt look large men share. Their long hair needed a wash. Both wore untucked, plaid flannel shirts and leather deck slippers. They could have been twins.

Lilly was quiet but not meek. She groused at her cousins.

"I live here too. He is my guest and he is welcome here. If this is a problem for you, we can talk to Appa Niki," Lilly said.

Tukok seemed a bit stunned and backed down.

After Lilly left the room, Niki arose with some difficulty and shook Snow's hand. Snow took an immediate liking to the man. He could sense wisdom, kindness, and humor in Niki's presence.

Niki bore a distinct resemblance to a walrus. That image would always stick in Snow's mind. Niki's head had been shaved, but now the hair was about an eighth-inch thick, a mixture of gray and white. His head was very large, and he had a prodigious double chin and large, beefy lips. He was a large man, with distinctly Native features.

Snow and Niki talked of Togiak and fishing. Snow displayed great deference to Niki. Snow always showed respect to elders, which had gained him a measure of acceptance by the locals, who held elders in great esteem. Niki had heard of the plane crash and subsequent killing of the great brown bear by Snow. He asked about it. Snow took a risk and unbuttoned his pants to show Niki the scar above his thigh.

Niki put on his glasses and motioned for Snow to come closer to the lamp so he could more closely inspect the scar. Niki had a smile on his lips. He took off his glasses and pulled himself to his feet. Snow shuffled back a step to allow him room. Elder Wasillie then exposed himself to Snow, showing him a series of white scars on his large, surprisingly white ass. The scars were old but still impressive and quite obviously claw marks.

Snow could not help himself and laughed out loud. Niki pulled his pants back up and they both sat down and chuckled.

"How you get yours?" asked Snow.

"Working on the boat. You know, I'm lying down under the boat. On the beach. So I suddenly got whacked. Real big whack, hurt like crazy."

"Bear?" asked Snow.

"Eee! Don't say why he whack me. Maybe just being bear. I crawl under and waved a stick at him. I had my hammer too," Niki said, waving his arms and ducking his head a bit to animate the story. "He's not really that interested anyways! So I did not fight the bear. Just saying hi." Niki smiled at the last bit. "Not like your bear, I think."

"Eee, my bear was definitely interested. He pushed me down from the back," Snow said. He had later learned that the bear was a boar, a male. "I hoped, you know, he would just go away. But he turned and charged me." Niki listened intently. "Surprised me that the bear did that."

"Eee. Sometimes when they first wake up they're very hungry and aggressive," said Niki.

"I was lucky. I mean, he could have killed me for sure. He took a break and it gave me a chance to get my gun out. Even then, I was lucky; he could have killed me after I shot at him, but he ran off."

Snow pulled his chair closer to Niki; they were sitting almost knee to knee by the fireplace in the living room.

"Have you heard about an ancient elder named Wasillie from Togiak?" asked Snow.

"Eee! Wasillie in Togiak. Long time ago. A great elder, Motok Wasillie, met the first white men. The white men hunt whale on the big water. Big boat came to Togiak. First white men in Alaska. How do you know about Motok?" Niki looked impressed.

Snow was fascinated. He told Niki what he had been aching to tell someone since the grizzly attack. "Kinka of the Little People told me about Motok Wasillie and the white whaler."

Niki's eyebrows shot up, causing a wrinkle chain reaction on his forehead. Niki then smiled in a wise way. He rocked back and forth meditatively with his hands on his nose. He lifted his hands to the top of his head and brought them down over his face, rubbing all the way, sounding like sandpaper. This was clearly Niki's habit when he was thinking.

Niki told Snow that he never met a Little People, or *Enukins*, as they were called by the Native people. He had heard the legend of Kinka the Kind. There were many stories of the Little People, and Niki believed them.

Niki asked if it was really true that Snow met Kinka.

"I thought it might be a dream. But part of me knew it was real. He saved me. I was in bad shape and cold. Kinka found me after the bear attack and led me to a cabin. He saved me for sure," said Snow.

Niki sat back and smiled as he listened to the story. Snow showed the scar on his shoulder and Niki again examined it closely before he said, "You are blessed or very fortunate. It is either very good luck or very bad when someone meets the Little People. The Enukin. They are legend of our tribe. Lots of stories, but no one is sure where Enukin come from.

"They seem like they are spirit world to me. I mean, from stories I heard, they seem more from spirit world than our world. The way they come and go so easy, so quick," Niki continued. "There are stories of Enukin helping hunters who have been lost. There are others who say the Little People made them lost. I heard stories that they can help you, but they might trick you, too. I think they are left over from another time."

Niki told Snow that he must be a special sort and fortunate. He thought it was a huge omen for Snow. Kinka was the greatest, wisest and kindest of the Little People.

"You must be good luck!" Niki said.

Snow and Niki sat for a few minutes, the silence thick with thoughts and meaning.

■ ■ ■

The fire in the hearth crackled. Lilly had been watching and listening from the door to the den. She was pretty sneaky when she wanted to be. She could stay silent and immobile for minutes. She could almost disappear. She was very impressed by all this. Not by the talk of the Little People, so much, but by how Niki seemed to connect with and embrace the gussok Snow. She had not seen her grandfather warm up to anyone like this, particularly a non-Native.

The spell was broken. Snow's cop sense finally kicked in and he looked over at Lilly. She was wearing forest-green corduroy pants with a colorful, flowered vest over a brilliantly white blouse. Her black hair hung loose, almost to her waist. She had her arms crossed. She was petite, neat and clean. Snow thought she was stunning, and the white shirt and colored vest highlighted her brown skin dramatically.

She was about to duck away but did not. Instead she looked Snow in the eye. They had a connection, and neither wanted to break it by looking away. This time it was his turn to wryly smile. Instead of being ashamed at being caught, she candidly returned his smile and went back to the kitchen. She added a little pert swish to her backside as she turned.

Tukok enter the room and consumed much of the light. Whatever cloud of good feeling was in the air instantly evaporated. He asked Snow to help him out at the shed. Snow bowed to Niki, said thank you, and left with Tukok.

"Come see me again," Niki said to Snow.

In the metal shed, Tukok and Pukok confronted Snow. He was caught off guard but quickly girded himself for whatever might come. He knew these two large men were more than a match for him physically. But he thought their intent was to try and frighten him off, as bullies do.

"What cher doing here? We don't want you here," said Tukok with some menace.

"Not welcome," said Pukok, with less conviction than Tukok.

"Not here to cause trouble. I am interested in your cousin Lilly. But I have respect for her, and I respect her family." Snow spoke calmly. "I also respect the Native ways and know you guys are just trying to protect your cousin. I have good intentions with Lilly. If she asks me to come here again, I will come here again."

He displayed no fear to them and hoped they could not smell it on him. He did not want to fight, because he would lose. But he would fight if he had to.

"You feisty, Snow? Like a schnauzer dog?" Tukok laughed. Snow was unsure if it was humor or derision.

Tukok was the aggressive one and stepped close to Snow.

"You hurt her, I hurt you," Tukok said low and slow. He stepped past Snow, who made room for him. Pukok gave him a look that seemed to indicate that he was not against Snow.

Snow left the shed just as Lilly came out of the house. He said nothing to her about this little confrontation. He knew if he said something to Lilly, who in turn talked to Tukok and Pukok, he would lose face with them.

"Ready to go?" he asked.

They had dinner at Miguel's restaurant, which had old-fashioned red-checkered tablecloths. A lit candle inside a red glass vase sat on each table. The floor was plywood, but the food was good. Even though he felt close to Lilly, the conversation was sparse at dinner. The air was too electric to support small talk.

When it was over, she gave him a ride to the airport in her dented old red Honda Civic with the spiderweb of cracks on the windshield. That was the fate of all windshields in the bush, with the abundance of rocky roads and the paucity of spare parts.

She smiled at him before he got on the plane, and his heart melted. She was the most beautiful person he had ever met, and he would endure anything to be with her. He would just figure out a way to win over the twins.

■ ■ ■

After he got back to Togiak, Snow drove back to the station and made peace with his coffee mug. He had about half a cup of white-sugared coffee in him when the mayor entered the office.

Major Moses Moon was a man among men. He had strong Native features, confidence, and the carriage of a man in charge, a man not to be trifled with. He could speak passionately and eloquently as well. *This is man destined for the Alaska Senate,* thought Snow. He rose and offered Mayor Moses a cup of coffee, which the mayor waved off.

"Come quick. It's bad."

CHAPTER 6

THE CRIME

Mayor Moses wanted to take his vehicle, but Snow insisted. They drove in Snow's pickup to Bullshit Bob Pollack's residence. When they got there, they were greeted by a city employee known as Joe the Waterman.

Joe's job was to deliver water to people who were not connected to the water and sewer utilities, which was about half the town. Those people had water tanks that they got refilled once or twice a week. For sewage needs they either had a "gray water" tank that got pumped out by the "honey wagon," or they had a simple honey bucket they emptied themselves.

Bullshit Bob had the water-tank-and-honey-bucket system. The house was out of town, on the ridge where Snow had admired the caribou earlier. Bullshit Bob shared his home with Buck Nelson, a troublemaker and small-time criminal.

Bullshit Bob was a friendly drunk who had migrated to Alaska many years ago for a life away from law and order. He was one of those who were a half-bubble off, for sure, but friendly and mostly harmless. The "Bullshit" nickname was hung on him years ago by drinking buddies, because Bob's stories had a loose relationship with facts.

Buck Nelson was a different matter. He showed up in Togiak about two years ago. He was a bad seed—everyone knew. Nelson was an outlaw pure and simple. He struck Snow as a predator, and a violent one.

There were rumors that Buck Nelson kept Bullshit Bob in illegal alcohol and in turn he had access to Bob's fishing permits. He certainly fished Bob's permits, but Bob was not complaining—not to Snow anyway. He thought that Nelson was a bully, intimidating people with his bluster and sophisticated ways bred in bigger cities. But there was nothing for Snow to hang his hat on.

Snow did a criminal history check on Nelson after he heard the bootlegging rumors. He saw that Nelson had a couple arrests: one for assault and one for possession of narcotics. Both had been reduced from felonies to misdemeanors. Snow thought Nelson was destined for more jail time; he had the look.

Snow disliked Nelson at first sight, which was very unusual for Snow. He usually gave people the benefit of the doubt until they proved otherwise. And it didn't take Nelson long to do just that.

Snow remembered the first time he spoke to Nelson. Snow had walked into the AC store to get a few things. He stopped at the big bulletin board at the front to peruse the homemade ads advertising things for sale and the like. Buck Nelson was on the pay phone about five feet away, talking.

"I know you are fucking trying to listen to me, cop. Why don't you fucking leave? I was here first," Nelson hissed at Snow.

Snow had been taken aback by the outright and open hostility from Nelson, and it instantly raised his blood pressure.

"I will leave when I'm done looking at the board," Snow responded evenly, like they were talking about the weather. Snow had learned not to show emotion, anger specifically. It worked to avoid escalating situations but also to send a message to bad guys: *Your tough-guy thing is nothing to me.* Snow had stood there for several long minutes looking at the board while Nelson had his hand over the phone, giving him the death stare.

Joe the waterman had arrived at Bullshit Bob's and opened the trapdoor at the side of the house, opened the tank, and put the hose in the house. Joe began to pump the water. While he was waiting for the tank to fill, he looked inside and saw Bob's legs raised like he was sitting in a chair. Something about the way he looked gave Joe the willies. Joe could also see what looked like blood on the floor. Joe retracted the water hose, hopped into his truck and called for help on his town radio. The mayor responded and immediately went to get Snow.

While waiting for help to arrive, Joe knocked on door, but no one answered. He did not know what to do, so he waited. The chief and mayor radioed to make sure someone from the clinic was on the way.

Once they arrived, Snow found the outside door to the arctic entry—or "cunnychuck"—open, but the inside door was locked tight. Snow went around the house and looked through the dusty window. Mayor Moses stayed with Joe, trying to calm him and get a better account of what he saw.

The chief saw what Joe had—Bullshit Bob in a recliner, legs up. There were many dark splotches and a large pool on the floor. *Joe the Waterman was right. Sure looks like blood.*

Snow went back to the front door. He backed up and gave it his best kick right by the knob. *Not like TV at all,* he thought. He tried the shoulder but could tell by the sheer immobility of the door and the pain in his shoulder that it was secured by a two-by-four or something similar. This was not uncommon. It was bear country after all. Also, pesky neighbors looking for a stash of hooch were prone to break in, especially when liquored up.

Snow went around the back. There was no back door. *All the windows are up too high to crawl through*, he thought as he quickly surveyed the house.

"Joe, you got a tool? A bar or sledge or something heavy?" Snow called.

"Eee!" Joe said, which was his way of saying "yes."

Joe the Waterman produced a four-foot lead pipe he kept on the back of the battered and dusty old green 500-gallon Ford one-ton along with some chains and various other tools he had found useful over the years. Joe was kind of slow, but he was not stupid. Snow took the lead pipe from Joe and hefted it. *Perfect.* A big length of pipe was very handy to have around.

Snow and Moses approached the door. Snow rammed the region of the doorknob, but nothing budged. *Damn.* Just as he thought, the door was secured with something heavy. He took out the hinges with a few whacks of the pipe and was able to lever the door open a crack, enough to squeeze through at the bottom. When he got in, he knocked the two-by-four out of the homemade wooden U-brackets ten-penny-nailed to the studs around the door. He had a moment of grim satisfaction that he had been right about the two-by-four.

Snow walked into the main room. As soon as he saw Bullshit Bob's condition, he told Moses and Joe to stay put. Moses stopped in his tracks as soon as he saw Bob, which was right inside the doorframe. Joe ran into Moses's back. Moses gave Joe a pretty good shot with his elbow.

"Jesus, Joe, I ain't your girlfriend. Back up!" Moses commanded.

Joe backed off maybe a centimeter while both men continued to look at poor old Bullshit Bob, whose guts were hanging out like an untucked red flannel shirt.

"Just don't step in here or touch anything," Snow told them firmly.

Snow did a quick check of the house. He took out his sidearm like he was trained to do, but he somehow knew no one was there, and he was right. He came back to the living room, which had a bare two-by-six plank floor. Snow told Moses to see if he could raise Stanley Beans and Nasruk Toovak. He was going to need some help.

"By the way, you can tell the clinic to cancel the call," Snow hollered with some sarcasm over his shoulder. *Like they were in any rush*, thought Snow. *Sure hope I ain't dying some day and have to rely on them to save me.*

Moses saw the rifle at Bob's feet. It was an old hunting rifle, probably a 30.06 Remington. There was a lot of blood on the floor. Bob must have shot himself in the high gut area. A lot of people ended their lives in the bush, either from depression or alcoholism or both. Most offed themselves with a gun when they were drunk. *Drink makes brave. Bob was brave most of the time,* Moses thought.

Moses was used to hunting, killing and skinning animals, so the blood did not bother him. Bob's face, though, had a look of horror. His eyes were wide open and his mouth was agape. Bob's skin had turned the same gray shade as most of his hair.

Bullshit Bob's gut was torn open, mostly on his right side, and some of his guts had spilled out like caribou sausage hanging to dry, speckled black with dried blood. Lots of torn flesh—a mess of Bob, for sure. The old chair was soaked black with blood. It looked he had been dead for a day or so, in Moses's estimation. He had seen enough and told Snow he would get some help.

He turned and bumped into Joe, beak to beak, knocking Joe's hat cockeyed. Moses had forgotten Joe was still standing about an inch behind him, goggling at the gore.

"Jezzus, Joe! Move the fuck out the way, will ya!"

Snow was alone with Bullshit Bob's body for a good thirty minutes before Stanley Beans arrived. Snow did not have any rubber gloves with him. He pulled out his well-worn calfskin gloves from his back pocket and slid them on. He pulled his right glove back off and checked Bob, who was cold as stone but not stiff. He was loose and pliable, starting to smell. Snow, too, had noticed the horrified look in Bob's pasty eyes and the shape of his mouth.

Snow carefully stepped around the body. Things did not feel right. *Why would Bob gut-shoot himself with a rifle? Why not the head?* And then there was the wound. Snow was no expert, but to him it looked Bob was shot from a foot or two away, judging by the blood spatter and size of the wound. *How did you do that with a rifle? You could use your toe,* he guessed, *or a stick or something.* He looked around but did not see anything on the floor that Bob could have used for that purpose. And Bob was wearing boots.

Snow saw the spent shell casing off to Bob's left. He stepped around the shell and checked the rest of the small house. There was no back door, which was not unusual—doors cost money. There were only three big windows. Windows cost even more than doors. There was a window in each of the two bedrooms and the one in the living area that Snow had peered through. Snow checked each. They were cranked shut, dust caked, and looked like they had not been opened for months. There was no other way out of the house except the trapdoor to fill the water tank that Joe had peeked into.

Snow went to the closet off the kitchen, where the 200-gallon metal water tank and water heater were stored. On his tippy toes, he looked on top of the tank. The trapdoor was still hanging open, letting in some light. Snow saw a smudged footprint on the tank. The footprint was indistinct, but he could probably get the size, maybe more. The footprint did not look like the kind that might be left when the lid was on the floor and someone stepped on it. It looked like someone had pushed off and smeared the print, like they would if they were climbing out the trapdoor.

"Hey, Chief Snow," Nasruk Toovak announced himself and entered.

Nasruk Toovak was an impressive man. He was about six foot two, lean, and strong. He had a commanding presence, which spoke of his many years as a village public safety officer (VPSO). A VPSO was essentially an unarmed constable for the villages. Even though Togiak now had a police department, Toovak continued in his role as VPSO.

Toovak and Snow got along well and had divided up the workload for the village. They even shared the office space at the department. Snow handled all criminal cases, which was just fine with Toovak, who at this point in his life did not want to deal with any conflict or paperwork. Toovak was happy to help out, though, and was extremely steady and forthright.

"Suicide?"

"Could be, Nasruk. But something's not right about it. You think Bob would do this? Like this?" Snow asked Toovak.

"I don't know. He was drunk most of the time. People say he sold his permits to Buck for booze. Maybe."

"What you think?" Toovak asked Snow.

Snow did not look directly at him. He spoke, hands on hips, looking around the room. "I wonder where Buck Nelson is. Upriver?"

"He has a fish camp upriver and another set-net cabin on the outside," Toovak replied. "What you think? Buck do this?"

Snow looked at Toovak. "I don't know, Nasruk. I have some problems with this thing."

Stanley Beans abruptly entered the house, tripped, and fell over the doorjamb into Toovak, who had a look of extreme annoyance. Stanley hung onto Toovak to maintain his balance and looked at Snow peevishly. The bumbling Beans had broken Snow's reverie.

Snow requested that Beans and Toovak stay at the scene while he went back to the station to call Trooper Dick. For Stanley Beans's benefit, he said to them both not to touch anything.

■ ■ ■

Snow was lucky to get in touch with Trooper Dick. Often Dick and his partner were out of the office. Snow considered himself even luckier when Trooper Dick said that one of them would be over in an hour or two. Snow thought they might not make it over until the next day, if at all.

"Bring a box, Dick," Snow said.

"Shit, Snow! Of course Bullshit Bob Pollack shot himself. Why would anyone shoot that old drunk bastard! People shoot themselves all the time here. That's just the way it is; you know that. That's life in the bush. Life's a bitch, then you shoot yerself!" Trooper Dick opined with authority.

Trooper Dick was looking to open and close this death quickly. But if the evidence suggested something nefarious, he'd do his job. *He is a good a cop, but he is getting long in the tooth and a bit tired*, Snow thought.

Trooper Dick hung up the phone. *Chief Snow is too fresh on the job,* he thought. *Give him a few more years and he won't go looking under every rock for a worm. Still, he is pretty good for a village cop and has some sense.*

Snow was also prone to be too easy with the locals at times. He was going to "go Native" after a while. *Then he'll be useless,* Trooper Dick thought. He'd seen good cops go soft many times before.

Trooper Debbie Roop and Trooper Dick arrived in the blue plane about an hour and a half later. *Record time,* thought Snow. The trio worked the scene. There was no note to be found—not that anyone expected one. No one was sure if Bullshit Bob could even read.

Trooper Dick did not want to take the body for an autopsy. He knew, as did Snow, that the medical examiner in Anchorage did not like flying bodies around unless he was damn sure it was a suspicious death. It cost tens of thousands of dollars to fly bodies all over the state. Bodies examined by a coroner in the lower forty-eight would not get the same treatment in Alaska just based on the dollars and logistics. The occasional murder probably went unnoticed simply because there was no autopsy performed.

Trooper Dick agreed to take the body to Dillingham, where they could keep it on ice, and to pull some fluids. He could drop it off for burial on his next trip back this way.

There was not much evidence to collect. They took the gun and shell casing. At least that would make it to the crime lab even if the body didn't. Snow put the lid from the water tank in the back of his truck. Snow wanted to use a gel pack to lift the footprint and thought he might as well do it himself. *It does not look like a good print, and what will it prove anyway?*

They bagged the body and put it in the back of Toovak's pickup. At the plane, they put the body in a light aluminum box called a Zeigler case, which the troopers brought with them. The box made it easier to lift Bob in the plane than a droopy body bag would have. *Always thinking, those troopers.*

The two troopers made a half-hearted effort to peruse the crime scene, but they were tired, and this case seemed straightforward. After a few minutes talking about what Snow was going to do on his end to wrap up the suicide, the blue plane left town. Snow had been happy to see them come—the troopers were a great help—but was happier to see them go. He still had some things he wanted to check out before he put this case to bed.

Maybe Trooper Dick was right. Maybe this was just another suicide in the endless string of tragedies that was part of life in the bush. Sometimes there was so much death and pain out in the village that Snow did not know how people went on. *But there is a lot of good here, too,* he thought.

Snow had a notion that Nelson had a hand in Bullshit Bob's death. There was something in Bob's eyes.

Snow went looking for Nelson.

CHAPTER 7
THE WALRUS

The year was 1898 near Togiak, Alaska.

Tukok Toovak, who was the ancestor of Nasruk Toovak, looked out over the calm water toward the Walrus Islands in the hazy distance. An illusion made the islands appear to be floating above the water. He scanned the water's surface and the beach stretching to his right for any movement. He was looking for the walrus. A scout for his clan had spotted walrus near what would one day be called Cape Pierce, a bluff that rose several hundred feet above the water.

Toovak was the leader of this hunting party. He was considered an elder in his clan though only forty years of age. He was a good hunter and a wise man. At five feet eight inches, Toovak stood tall above his group. He wore his finest sealskin leggings over sealskin mukluks. He had a precious itchy wool sweater under his outer coat also made of sealskin. His raven hair was pulled back in a braid fashioned and adorned with small shells by his wife. Toovak had the starkly handsome, dark features of his clan, named *Toovak* after the caribou.

Toovak looked at his small group of men. They were too few.

Since the first whaling boat captained by Jonathan Shoemaker about thirty-five years earlier, there had been many other whalers. They had been welcomed by Toovak's people. Soon after the boats came the sickness. Wave after wave of sickness. Whole clans had been devastated. The stench of death was everywhere. For a time, the survival of the Native people in this region was in question. The spirits had deserted them. Tribes that had warred in the past now joined to survive.

First it had been the small pox, and that had been devastating. Later, there had been waves of the flu.

Where there had been thousands, now there were hundreds. Those that survived were not touched by the sickness, as if protected by magic. But the white men brought others things. Some good, some bad.

Toovak had a harpoon, a sharp steel blade attached with sinew at the point. He traded for the steel blade with whale oil and hides. The blades were magical, like the wool jacket he wore.

The rum that white men brought with them was also magical but in a demonic and dark way. When his people drank it, they were transfixed. Some claimed to see visions. Others became violent like animals. Many more became lethargic. They only wanted the drink and became indolent. They only hunted when they needed more rum. *This rum sickness erodes the spirit of my people,* thought Toovak. It seemed that the spirits not only abandoned his people but were also punishing them.

The burden on Toovak and the other elders was severe. Before the whalers, elders held council on rare occasions when a clan member could not abide by the common laws of the tribe. Once a generation or so, a tribal member would be banished. It was rare. Most tribal members would abide by the will of the people rather than risk being cast out from their world. Now it seemed none too rare. Elder councils met often, conferring and even passing judgment on those who had committed violence. Even with their decimated numbers, they could not tolerate violent acts or those who were so consumed by rum that they gave nothing to the tribe.

These were not easy decisions; they tested the elders. Some wanted to let the "rummies" or violators stay. Toovak did not— would not. He knew his heart and what was right. He knew that the rum was a curse to his people. The rum and what it wrought could not be tolerated.

In a radical and unprecedented move, the elders abolished the use of the rum or spirit drink. Never had the council exerted this measure of control. This chafed members of the tribe, who for the first time voiced dissension. It took all Toovak's strength and influence to impose the ban. The pull of the spirit drink was strong. He felt the battle had weakened his soul.

He surveyed the horizon again and made a decision. He gave the order to beach the boats. This was done easily as the boats were very light, made of caribou hide stretched tight over alder branches. The skins were sewn tight with caribou sinew and then coated with seal fat. The result was a nearly watertight, light, maneuverable watercraft. Today there were only three boats in the small hunting party of fifteen men. If they were successful, they would send word and more would come from the village if need be.

Tyriek Beans stumbled over a piece of driftwood as he helped move the boat. He fell flat, face-first in the sand. Toovak could not help but laugh at his good, bumbling friend. Tyriek was an ancestor of the brothers Frank and Stanley Beans.

"If we find the beach, you cannot fall, Tyriek. Or the walrus will mate with you!"

"No! He's too ugly even for a walrus!" one of the men said.

Tyriek Beans brandished his tiny but sharp steel knife with its caribou horn handle.

"Eee!" Tyriek shook his head, meaning "not so fast." "If he pokes at me with his *oosik*, I will cut it off." He pulled the giant, imaginary walrus penis with one hand high in the air and slashed horizontally with the other. Everyone chuckled or shook their heads.

Toovak fell in with the others and helped haul the skin boat above the tide line. Then he drew the men in around him. He outlined his audacious plan. It was clear they approved the risky idea. The rewards would be great if they were successful. Not only would they harvest a huge supply of walrus for the tribe, but they would also gain tremendous fame. Songs would be sung. Dances would describe the hunt for generations.

The men headed out together toward the point.

Toovak, with his sharp eyes, had seen movement on the cape. When they got closer, they got stealthy. Toovak and Tyriek climbed to a high point while the others held back. What Toovak saw was perfect for his plan.

He came back down and they prepared for the attack. Usually, they would attack a walrus high on the beach, surround it, and hope to mortally wound it before it got one of the hunters. Other times, they would harpoon it with a seal bladder attached to a rope made of sinew. They followed the walrus, and when it surfaced they would repeatedly spear it. This was very similar to how they hunted beluga or humpback whale. Both could be successful—but dangerous—ways to hunt a walrus.

Dozens of walruses had hauled out high on the beach at the cape. Some had even climbed up the gentle inland slope. The walruses saw the approaching group of strange-looking creatures running along the water's edge. The herd began to rumble toward the water.

Those highest on the slope undulated away from the others

in their strange but surprisingly speedy way. The tribe had split the group as planned! The hunters ignored the walruses heading into the water, instead giving chase to those heading up the slope. The hunters were gaining.

Tyriek Beans ran close to one of the walruses. It suddenly wheeled and scooped at him with its three-foot-long ivory tusks. The walrus caught Beans neatly and he flew high in the air. A nearby hunter charged at the walrus with a lance just as it was about to gore Tyriek, who had landed and crumpled on the sand and grass. The walrus wheeled away and took off in the direction of the others.

The hunters chased about ten walruses up the slope. Several peeled away and tumbled down the slope onto the beach. Toovak hollered to ignore those that had fallen and chase the last up the hill.

At the apex of the cape, a few hunters led by Toovak cut off the final group of seven. Toovak screamed, as did the others. The walruses veered hard to the left and off the bank. Instead of a nice, gentle roll down to the beach, they fell some sixty feet off the small cliff, bouncing several times before landing on the boulders below.

It worked! All the men screamed for joy as they saw the walruses dead or dying below them on the rocks. They stood and admired their work, recounting the great hunt. But Tyriek! What of Tyriek?

Toovak ran back to where Tyriek had been tossed. Tyriek was lurching dazedly toward them, covered in sand. The men gathered round. It was determined that he was okay, so they all laughed as several recounted Tyriek's unexpected flight through space. Several were already demonstrating potential dance moves.

Tyriek looked indignant as he brushed the sand off his person. But he soon laughed too. The hunt was the most successful in memory, and soon they would be venerated by all.

■ ■ ■

Charlie Johnson came to in a fog. He hurt all over. He raised his head and looked around. He recognized that he was in his hunting cabin upriver from the village. He lay his head back down and tried to remember. He could recount that he recovered the last five bottles of his latest alcohol cache. He sold two bottles in the village and helped drink them. He had saved three for himself.

He had been drinking with Bullshit Bob and the Beans boys. Everything had been fine until Buck Nelson arrived. Charlie did not like Nelson. They were bootlegging competitors, but lots of people sold alcohol on occasion, so their rivalry was not just that. There was something else. Nelson was a user and greedy. Charlie did not like the way Nelson took advantage of Bullshit Bob. Bob was a drunk and a gussok, but Charlie liked him. He had lived in the village for years and even took care of Charlie's cousin Nancy before she died. Bullshit Bob and Nancy had lived together, though they never married. Since her death, Bob drank even more, like he was trying to drink himself to death.

Charlie remembered Nelson coming to Bullshit Bob's shack last night. *Fat and ugly,* Charlie thought. *A true ugly white scoundrel.* He looked at Nelson with disdain. Despite his belly, Nelson was powerful and agile. He was smelly, too, and looked as though he never bathed.

Charlie Johnson despised Nelson because he instilled fear in people. That was usually Charlie's thing. Nelson had been in a variety of one-sided fights during his time around Togiak and had been merciless in his beatdown of the drunks he fought. He was smart about who and when he fought. He knew how to use his fists. And when he had the advantage, he was not afraid to take it.

Nelson looked upon Charlie with equal scorn.

"See you have some of your usual overpriced rotgut," he said to Charlie, not even showing the respect of calling him by name.

There was immediate tension in the air between the burly white interloper and Charlie Johnson, the wild and scary local boy. A showdown was coming; it was just a matter of when and where.

"Better than buying from a gussok! Right boys?" Charlie explained with a laugh. Charlie threw in the "right boys" to suggest that, when push came to shove, Charlie was one of the village people and Nelson was not. Nelson was an outsider and a gussok.

"People will buy from whoever has the jugs at the best price," Nelson said to no one in particular.

Charlie was nothing if not smart and tough and dangerous. If it came to a straight fight with Nelson, he could win. But it would not be easy, and he was not interested in getting bloody tonight. He was more interested in the drink. He could not lose face, though.

"Go drink with your friends then, Buck, if you have any," Charlie said genially, with hate and wild unpredictability in his eyes. *If it's now, so be it,* thought Charlie.

Nelson reassessed. He did not acknowledge Charlie again but spoke to the small group.

"I have work to do while you girls sit around and drink."

It was said in jest, and the tension eased in the room. The men began to talk drunkenly among themselves again. Nelson gathered up a rifle and some things around the house. Charlie kept a wary eye on him until Nelson left.

Afterwards, Charlie took a four-wheeler to recover one more bottle at the urging of the others. He felt very good—high and warm—as he drove fast. He made sure to leave himself one bottle no matter what. He would need it the next day to recover. He did not remember leaving Bullshit Bob's cabin after that bottle or coming home.

Charlie checked and saw with relief that his skiff was parked on the bank of the river. He noticed what looked like blood on his hands. He looked but found no apparent wounds. There looked like some dried blood on his jeans. *Oh well. Mine,* he thought.

Charlie had been suffering recently from memory lapses. He wasn't sure of the cause, but it was probably from being drunk most of the time. He had been through too many blackouts to count. The scary part was that he sometimes drove or fought but had no recollection when he awoke. One time, he stayed drunk for almost a week and ended up in jail. For biting off his cousin's eyebrow.

Charlie did not end up in jail long over the eyebrow. Another time, Charlie was locked up for ramming a bunch of boats in a torrid incident in the middle of the Naknek River up north. Some gussoks had destroyed his nets on the beach. They had done it out of jealousy, he was sure. They were out on strike for higher prices, but Charlie had continued to fish. He was a scab to those on strike. And twice a day, those fishermen on strike would watch him drive by to deliver his catch to the tender, his boat loaded down with salmon. The fishing was very good with all the boats on the beach.

Some of the fishermen got tired of watching Charlie get rich while they were going broke. They poured battery acid on all of his nets. When Charlie came to the beach he went crazy. He jumped into his main fishing boat, a heavy old wooden thirty-two-footer with a steel skid plate, and rammed as many boats as he could. One of the fishermen retaliated, ramming Charlie's boat, the *Taku,* while he was on it, screwing it into the water and sinking it.

Charlie had leaped off the *Taku* onto the boat of the man who rammed him. In a vicious fight, Charlie wound up on the floor of the boat with a large, sharp knife to his throat. The man's daughter prevented him from slitting Charlie's throat. Charlie had been hog-tied and delivered to a tender, where he was placed under arrest by the Coasties. Charlie did not remember anything but waking up in a cell, which seemed to be happening more frequently.

■ ■ ■

Chief Snow cruised with Toovak in his covered metal skiff. Snow had decided to head upriver to talk with Buck Nelson, and Toovak agreed to give him a lift.

The Togiak River was a mile wide at the mouth but quickly constricted, intensifying its flow. Toovak knew the river well and cruised at top speed. Buck Nelson's fish camp was not too far. There was a summer fishing lodge another ten miles after that. Fishing or hunting shacks dotted the banks for a ways after the lodge, but then there was just wilderness. The country was nearly unpopulated. They passed a boat—Charlie Johnson heading to town.

Snow met with Buck Nelson at his shack. Toovak stayed with the boat. Snow felt some comfort knowing Toovak was there.

"What do you want?" Nelson spat at Snow. He did not seem to be surprised to see the chief.

"Just making some routine checks. Haven't been up this way in a while."

"I don't believe you, and even if something was going on, I don't talk to pigs." Nelson turned to walk away.

"Where were you yesterday?" Snow said, agitated by the attitude. *Probably been drinking,* the chief thought.

"You don't hear too good, I guess. Unless you have a warrant, get off my land," Nelson pushed.

"Bullshit Bob, your *partner*, is dead. I thought you might want to know. Unless you already stole everything he has." Snow regretted that as soon as it came out of his mouth. He hated when his mouth got ahead of his brain.

Instead of getting pissed like Snow expected, Buck Nelson started talking like a jailhouse lawyer, all calm and matter-of-fact.

"Everything between Bullshit Bob and me was strictly legal and by the book. Everything was signed and notarized. Bob sold me some things, but it was because he wanted to sell and I was buying. I have all the paperwork." He sounded like he was giving testimony in court, right down to the contrite expression.

Snow recovered and politely asked Nelson where he was the day before. Nelson told him he had been to Bullshit Bob's house to get some things yesterday afternoon and who had been in the house. Then he had come upriver and spent the night.

"See anybody up here last night?" Snow asked.

"I'm done talking." Nelson turned and went into the cabin.

"That went well," Snow told Toovak sarcastically on the ride back into Togiak. "One curious thing; Buck never asked how Bullshit Bob died."

"Eee! Holy shit!" Toovak said, eyebrows raised.

■ ■ ■

Chief Snow thought about Charlie Johnson and Buck Nelson, his two suspects in Bullshit Bob's death. Buck Nelson seemed more likely. Charlie just didn't seem right for this one.

Charlie Johnson was just eighteen when he got his fishing permit. It was a drift permit. His father, Cliff Johnson, had given it to him through his mother. Charlie hated Cliff even more for doing it, because it seemed like a paltry inheritance from a man who owned so much. Charlie got an old wooden boat from his father, too—his first boat. It was a green bow picker he named the *Taku*. The little boat did not draw much water, so he could nose around in the shallow water. He fished where others would not or could not go. He was daring and smart.

Charlie seemed fearless and took chances—well-calculated risks based on instinct and local knowledge. He had a feel for the water, wind and tides. He did not mind angering people and had developed a hatred for white people even though he was part white. What they represented, anyway. He saw them as profiteers, users. They came in the summer and took the fish and money, then left. Charlie embraced his Native heritage.

Charlie bought a new, large boat the next year and again named it the *Taku*. This boat was his pride and joy. He could do things with the *Taku* that amazed people who did not know the area as well as he did. Even locals were impressed. He was ruthless when he fished. There were set boundaries called "lines" around the mouth of the Naknek, Egegek, and other rivers in Bristol Bay. These lines were hotly contested fishing grounds. Charlie developed a reputation as someone who would set his net right in front of yours with no hesitation or remorse. That was called "corking" another fisherman, and Charlie was a ruthless corker.

Charlie had built a cabin out near Johnson Hill. It was about ten miles from Naknek. There was a small freshwater creek nearby, where he could nose his boat in at high tide. He liked the spot because it was near the fishing grounds. He took his four-wheeler into town at night to go to the bar.

One night, he went to his father's bar, the Gin Mill. The bar was hopping on this summer night. The sun stayed up all night and the people did too. There was a fishing closure, so the bar was full of fisherman and workers from the Alaska Packers and Bumblebee Seafood canneries that were both within walking distance.

Most of the hundred or so people in the Gin Mill were men. There were a handful of women there, too, though. The women were highly sought after and occasionally fought over by the men. A woman might be considered average in terms of physical beauty in Anchorage, but supply was thin and demand high. Each woman was surrounded by a gaggle of men attending to every need and word. Even Mattress Mary had a group of would-be suitors.

Snow was in the bar that night, long before he was police chief. Snow enjoyed the Gin Mill. He liked to watch people. The crowd was rowdy as usual, mostly due to the lack of law enforcement. Brawls and cursing spilled into the streets. Snow was only eighteen and too young to drink at the time, but Cliff Johnson had a policy. If you were old enough to work in the bush, you were old enough to drink in his bar.

Several white fishermen from Oregon were plotting at the bar, forming a game plan for Charlie Johnson, who was holding court by the pool table. Charlie, he was brash and cocky. He liked to tell stories of his fishing exploits, especially to the humiliation of gussok fishermen. These three men were hard, strong fishermen, toughened by salt and hard work. Young Charlie had corked one of them. Bold and bulletproof with alcohol, they sought to teach the young Native boy a lesson.

The three men closed in around Charlie, rudely elbowing his audience away. The look in their eyes and their manner discouraged the others from saying anything. All three wore leather deck slippers and flannel or wool shirts. The ringleader was a man they called Captain Crunch because of his propensity to ram unfriendly boats with his bow during the combat-fishing near the line. Crunch had fists the size of grapefruits.

The three had Charlie in a corner by the pool table. Captain Crunch was the mouthpiece and out front. His big fists were hanging loosely at his sides like a crane's headache balls. One of three had picked up a pool cue. He motioned people who had come close to watch to stay away.

Crunch admonished Charlie for corking his friend and demanded an apology. Charlie was already pretty savvy for his age. He knew there was no way to avoid this fight. So he figured there was no reason to mince any words—not that he would have anyway.

He responded with a comment about the gussok fishermen not knowing how to fish and their lack of intestinal fortitude.

"You gussoks don't know how to fish," Charlie said, which was not the truth at all. These men, though not local, had fished all their lives around Astoria, Oregon. Now they all fished Bristol Bay in the summers. "You don't fucking belong here. Why don't you take your fat ass back where you came from."

Captain Crunch had brawled before and was larger than Charlie. He swung for the body to ensure he would hit something and waded in after the punch. He liked things close so he could use his bulk and strength. Charlie fought back like the wild man he was, but they got him on the floor anyway. At one point Charlie managed to slip on top of Crunch. He bit off the tip of Captain Crunch's nose. One of the other men cracked Charlie over the shoulder with a pool cue.

Captain Crunch rolled Charlie off him while he screamed, "The half-breed bit me!"

All three put the boots to Charlie, who was half-conscious on the floor, blood streaming from an open cut above his ear. He curled into a fetal position.

Snow moved from the bar and watched the scene. He was fascinated but also sickened by the violence. When Charlie was defenseless on the floor, he found himself hollering and gesturing for them to stop. He got in the midst of them and grabbed Crunch by the arm and said to stop; they were going to kill him. Crunch pushed Snow aside and growled at him, but Snow came back in to try and stop them. Crunch wheeled on Snow as if to punch him but reconsidered. All three men stopped then, apparently satisfied and tired.

Snow saw a Native at the bar and told him to help. The young man raised his eyebrows to the ceiling and said, "Eee! *Hjuugh anuk* fuck *unku* Charlie shit!" Which meant God knew what, but he came right down and helped.

Frank N Beans and Snow dragged Charlie Johnson out of his father's bar. His father had watched the scene but not intervened. He was still thinking about it when Snow stepped in to stop it. He felt relieved. *Maybe Charlie will learn something, for Christ's sake,* he thought.

Outside, Charlie came around some. He pushed Snow and Frank away.

"Leave me the fuck alone!"

Charlie hopped on his four-wheeler and tore off. He came back a couple hours later in his Ford pickup. He positioned his truck perpendicular to the front of the bar, gunned the engine, and rammed the bar. He backed up a few feet and smashed into the bar again, wood splinters flying. Cliff Johnson rushed to the window, looked out and cursed.

"Fucking Charlie!"

But he did not go outside. He hollered at one of his workers, Whitie, to stop Charlie. Whitie, pale under his chronic acne and mop of greasy hair, stammered something in response. Cliff handed him the shotgun as the front of the bar crashed, thundering inward a few inches.

Whitie ran outside with the 12-gauge shotgun in his hands. Whitie was skinny and all of 140 pounds of young, gutless white boy. Charlie popped out of the truck and stalked toward Whitie until the gun was pressed against his chest. Young Whitie was shaking with fear.

"DO IT! SHOOT ME! GUSSOK MOTHERFUCKER!" Charlie's face was swollen horribly. Tears rolled down his face even as he screamed. He whipped the gun out of Whitie's hands and smacked him with the stock in one smooth motion. Then he poked Whitie viscously with the barrel.

"Don't point a gun at me unless you mean to use it!"

Charlie looked like he was thinking about shooting the gun. Snow came out of the the bar and called to Charlie, "Don't do it, Charlie. Whitie's not worth it."

"What the fuck do you know about what it is worth to me?" Charlie said, almost a sob.

CHAPTER 8
THE VISIT

Back in Togiak, Snow talked to Frank and his brother Stanley Beans. Both confirmed that Buck Nelson had been to Bullshit Bob's house that night, but they said they left Bullshit Bob's shortly after Nelson. They said Charlie Johnson was the only one there after that. The brothers also confessed that everyone had been drinking heavily.

"Guess I need to pay Charlie a visit," Snow said. He headed to Charlie's plywood shack on the river.

Charlie Johnson was unlike any man Snow had known. They met some years back around Naknek. Charlie could be charismatic and drew people like moths to a flame. He frightened yet attracted them. Meeting Charlie was like coming face-to-face with a big gray wolf when walking through the alders. You knew you should go the other way, but you really wanted to be friends with the wolf.

Charlie could sense fear just like a wolf, too. And he instilled it in anyone who crossed him. He was wild, tough, and capricious.

Snow remembered talking to a Native named Tom at the Gin Mill years back. When Charlie's name came up, Tom pulled the hair away from his face, exposing a scar above his right eye where his eyebrow should have been.

"That son of a bitch bit my eyebrow off!"

"How? I mean, how the heck does that happen? How does someone bite another guy's eyebrow off? I can't even imagine doing that," Snow said.

"It's not like you think," said Tom, taking the drink offer and settling into a fresh rum and coke. "I mean, we did not have a fight or anything. Charlie had just gotten off the river from the damn ramming thing. I was just gonna give him a ride up to his place, ya know. We were in the truck and he grabbed me by the head and bit my eyebrow off, and spit it on the floor of the truck," Tom said. "He was crazy. I think he was just out-of-his head drunk, in a blackout. I don't want anything to do with him ever again, and he's my cousin. Just too freaking crazy, man!"

"What'd you do after? I mean, what do you do after someone bites you?" asked Snow.

"I got the hell out of there. Just got away from him. I went back later and found my eyebrow, but they couldn't put it back on."

Despite Charlie becoming violent when drunk, Snow admired him in a strange way. Charlie was a free spirit and a lightning rod. He was legend in the villages for being a wild man as well as a good fisherman and outlaw.

Snow was not looking forward to arresting him again. The last time had been touch and go, but Charlie had agreed to come in without a fight.

Snow went to Charlie's place to pick him up on an assault charge about a year and a half ago. Toovak agreed to come with him, and they both expected trouble. When they made contact with Charlie at his shack, Charlie had gone wild, screaming and punching the walls but not making a move toward the lawmen.

He punched holes in the walls and bloodied his fists. Snow had pepper spray in his left hand and his right hand on his gun. Toovak carried a shotgun.

Like a switch had been flipped, Charlie settled down, and the chief asked him, "You done? Ready to go now?"

Charlie laughed and turned around with his hands behind his back. "Okay, little chief, I will let you arrest me now!"

"Careful." Toovak handcuffed Charlie.

Snow had never scrapped with Charlie, but that was lucky. Charlie had fought just about everyone else, and Snow had nightmares about Charlie biting him. The chief never really thought much about shooting anyone as part of the job, but that thought had crossed his mind with Charlie. He played the scenarios out as a kind of mental preparation. He would shoot Charlie if Charlie tried to bite him.

Snow banged on Charlie's door and heard some cursing as it opened.

"What the fuck do you want?"

Snow smelled booze on his breath. "Take it easy, Charlie. Just need to ask you a few simple questions."

"About what?" Charlie suddenly smiled big and easy, which was his way. His moods went up and down like a cork on the water.

"I think you know. Bullshit Bob's dead. Found him gutted in his house. The Beans boys said you were there hanging out. Two nights ago."

"Don't remember a damn thing. Don't even know for sure if I was there."

"What do you remember, Charlie?"

Charlie smiled again. Like many Natives, Charlie did not lie well or easily.

"Little Chief Snow, you think good for a small gussok cop," he said. There was something about the little chief that Charlie liked. Snow didn't treat him or other Natives like shit like the other cops. He was respectful. And he was fair.

"Pretty good," Snow said. "Not trying to trick you. Just trying to figure out what might have happened."

"I was pretty cooked. I don't know. I am sure Bob was alive when I left. I am sorry he's gone. He was a good gussok. He drink booze too much. Too much booze, like the rest of us, but he was good to my cousin Nancy. Treated her well. Always appreciated that," Charlie said.

Like other Natives out here, Charlie pronounced *booze* "boosh" and spoke slowly in a sing-song manner.

"I can't believe he would shoot himself like that," he slurred.

"What about Buck Nelson?" Snow asked.

"He is a cocksucker. Selling bad hooch all over. And he stole Bullshit Bob's permits. I should bite his fucking ear off!"

Charlie might just do it, too, Snow thought. He knew for a fact Charlie once bit a deckhand's lower lip off. It was later re-attached, though not well. It kind of hung there dog-eared.

"Why wouldn't Bullshit shoot himself?" Charlie huffed, now seeming to argue with himself. "He lost Nancy. He let his permits go to that fucker Nelson. He drank like he wanted to die."

"Maybe someone helped him along. Maybe a friend who did not want to see him suffer anymore," Snow said, eyeing Charlie's reaction.

"Maybe his fucking gussok partner Buck fucking Nelson who wanted everything Bullshit had!"

The interview didn't help much; it just confirmed that Charlie was there. He was still half-cooked, so Snow let it be for now.

■ ■ ■

Lilly Wasillie was nervous. She had never been to Togiak, but that was not the source of her angst. She had been to villages in the bush before, just not this one. *Exactly the same, but different,* she thought.

She had been thinking about Chief Snow ever since he visited her family. The thought of embracing him—or more—made her skin tingle and her heart flutter. She did not like to fly in the small bush planes and was glad when the Cessna 207 landed, kicking up a cloud of dust. She was met on the plane by the physician's assistant, a white man from the lower states. He would work six months or a year in the bush and then go down below, forever telling tales about his work in Alaska.

Alaska was in dire need of health care professionals. There were incentives for doctors or PAs to work in the state, especially the bush clinics. Not only could they pocket big money, they could also get forgiveness on parts of their student loans. Even with the incentives, many left quickly. They simply could not take life in the bush. No malls, movie theatres, golf courses, TV stations, Starbucks, or restaurants. Flush toilets were a luxury. Fresh milk, fruit and vegetables were hard to come by, expensive, and ready to go bad as soon as you got them. Not a lot of anything except wide-open spaces.

"I love it here!" the tall PA gushed. "I have plans to build a house out by the Cape."

"You should wait. Wait until you've lived here awhile," Lilly said.

"It's so peaceful. I want to learn to subsistence hunt and fish and build a house to live in. It's so different; none of the hustle bustle of the lower forty-eight."

"It's expensive," said Lilly. She knew that people from outside came out here and loved it for a while. After the newness wore off, things changed, perceptions shifted. Those who seemed to "love it" the loudest were often the first ones to bail out.

There were lots of oppressive health care issues to treat in these faraway places—hepatitis, TB, domestic violence, suicide, and fetal alcohol syndrome, all at rates way higher than most anywhere in the lower forty-eight. People would come in all starry-eyed and six months later they couldn't catch a plane out of here fast enough. Those that did stay, like Dr. Perez in Dillingham, were rare.

Nurses were in short supply, too. On occasion, Lilly ventured out to assist a doctor or PA or to look in on a previous patient. That was her excuse for visiting Chief Snow's village. Togiak did not have a doctor, just the visiting PA.

Dr. Perez suspected Lilly wanted to see Chief Snow but did not reveal his suspicions to Lilly or anyone else. He liked Lilly. She was a good nurse. She also knew how to keep her mouth shut, which was refreshing. She was Native as well, and he felt paternalistic toward her.

Lilly would stay at the clinic in Togiak. They had spare rooms with beds just for that purpose. When the PA told her that she could stay downstairs at the Round House, she blushed. She knew the PA was simply recommending it because others sometimes preferred to stay there. He knew nothing about her and Snow, she was sure. He was much too self-consumed.

The PA blathered on about the Round House, and how the chief of police lived upstairs. It was an old converted water tank, the PA explained, with multiple bedrooms downstairs.

"It's the coolest place to stay if you don't mind a cop living upstairs. You can see the fish jumping right out your window," he said.

"I don't want fish jumping out my window," joked Lilly.

Chief Snow came by the clinic to see Lilly within an hour of her arrival. He felt like a smitten teenager, his heart racing and armpits dampening. He spotted her in the hallway talking to a child. She was on her knees with the little girl, who was crying.

Lilly looked even more beautiful than before, if that were possible. She had her hair pulled back in a very thick braid.

Some wisps had escaped to hang on her forehead. She looked like an angel in blue scrubs.

Lilly spotted him watching her and gave him a tiny smile of acknowledgement. His heart skipped. She met him in the waiting area, still holding the little girl's hand. She stood so close to Snow that the usually stoic chief blushed.

Lilly told the girl that this was a police officer, and the girl, who had stopped crying, looked at Snow quizzically. Snow slipped out his flashlight and flashed it as a way to keep the girl interested. It worked.

"You want to go riding after work? We could have a picnic?" Snow whispered to Lilly as she kept an eye on the young girl, who had been simply scared and upset.

"You flirting with me, Chief? she whispered

"Maybe," he responded. "Is it working?"

"Maybe," she whispered and smiled.

"That sounds fun. I will get some food from the AC store we can take with us. Pick me up here," she said.

"See you later!" Snow said. He smiled at the girl and bent down to let her take a closer look at the light.

■ ■ ■

Snow jumped on his red Honda ATV and rode back to the station standing up with the wind in his face, which was his habit. The Honda 400 series was the ride of choice in this part of the world. They could go almost anywhere. The big spongy tires would drive right over rocks and small logs with no problems. They would even float, though not well enough to carry a rider. But you could float them across a stream if you were careful. Some models were big enough to haul a quarter of a caribou. Best of all, they were a blast to ride.

Lester Grimes was waiting at the office for Snow and followed him inside. Grimes's nickname was "Grimy," and for good reason. He rarely bathed, and even when he did he looked dirty. It was like the dirt was ground in and now a part of him. He worked for a local mechanic, which accounted for some of the grime. His old jacket was covered with grease. Grimy smelled like oil and tobacco, though not unpleasantly.

"What's up, Lester?"

Chief Snow always called him Lester, which made Grimy feel good.

"That little fucker JJ stole my steering wheel! I want him arrested!" Grimy sputtered.

"Have a cup of coffee? Tell me what happened."

Chief Snow handed Grimy a white Styrofoam cup. He always gave Grimy a throwaway. The grease and grime imbedded into the lines of his fingers smeared anything he touched. His coffee cup was greasy brown within minutes.

The police station had become a place to stop for coffee since Snow became chief. Snow liked the company and, being single, he was there most of the time. Having a steady stream of visitors also helped him learn what was happening around the village and in the bush. People liked to come by and shoot the breeze, especially when the snow was thick and temperatures frigid. It gave shut-ins something to do. Although the station was kind of dumpy, it was comfortable and warm. And there was a flush toilet, to boot.

But Grimy was there for a purpose today.

"You know my truck, the Ford F150 with the short bed?"

"Yup, it's usually parked right by your place, right?" Snow responded.

"Yeah, well, I had a custom-installed, chain-link chrome steering wheel, and it's gone." The description made it sound like quite the truck, which was not the case.

"Why do you think JJ took it?" Snow asked.

"Well, I saw it on his truck."

"Oh, well that's what they call a clue," Snow remarked dryly.

After listening to the story, Snow was pretty sure that JJ did in fact take Grimy's prized chain-link steering wheel. Snow was sure there was more to this story, though. Maybe it was part of a dope deal. Grimy, along with about half of the people in Togiak, occasionally smoked weed. Smoking pot was legal in Alaska, and Snow much preferred its mellowing effect on the locals over the violence and rage induced by booze. "If everyone smoked weed instead of getting liquored up, I'd be out of a job," Snow often said.

Snow thought Grimy's complaint was kind of silly. The steering wheel was on an ancient pickup that hardly ever ran. It was missing the window on the driver's side, and none of the lights worked. It was Grimy's summer truck. But it was important to Grimy.

"I been plannin' on fixing her up," said Grimy.

Snow decided to check things out and went to JJ's house. He had Grimy with him but made him stay in the truck. JJ became indignant.

"Why would I want his steering wheel?" A nice non-denial denial. "No way I took his steering wheel." JJ looked upset, but Snow felt like it was an act. JJ was upset, all right, but probably because the police were at his house and Grimy had ratted on him.

"That gussok Grimy owes me money anyway," JJ said.

Bingo, thought Snow.

"Maybe this is just a misunderstanding. I mean, maybe you thought you were never going to get your money, or maybe Grimy said you could borrow the steering wheel until you got your money. Is that what this was about? A misunderstanding because of the money Grimy owes you?" Snow asked JJ.

"Yeah, but I don't have his stupid steering wheel," JJ complained.

Oh, come on! thought Snow. "I know where it is. I saw it in your truck, outside. Come and look," Snow said to JJ, not rubbing it in too much. JJ was a terrible liar.

They went out to the truck and there it was, mounted on the steering column of JJ's truck. Snow made it clear he was not leaving until he got the chrome chain circle, which moved JJ along. There was a simple nut attaching it, and it popped right off.

"Next time, come and see me first, JJ. I don't want you to get in any trouble."

JJ agreed and that was that. Snow delivered the wayward steering wheel to Grimy with JJ in tow.

"Sorry, Grimy," JJ said like an embarrassed little boy.

"Grimy, JJ's done his part to make things right. Now you do your part. I understand you owe him some money."

Grimy nodded, reached into his grubby pocket, removed a crumpled twenty-dollar bill and slapped it into JJ's outstretched hand.

"Even."

■ ■ ■

Snow got back to the station only to be greeted by Mayor Moses.

"Don't forget tribal court. It starts at one," Moses reminded him. It was half past one already, so Snow figured he was right on time. Everything started a half hour or so late. *Village time,* he thought with a smile.

"I am on the way," the chief said to the mayor.

"Do you think this is a good idea? I mean, this school dispute is a pretty hot issue."

"Too late now. The elders can handle it. Let's go!"

Snow grabbed his file on the case and roared to the Senior Center on the ATV. Not because he was in a hurry—it was simply fun to roar around on an ATV. There were people milling outside as he braked and threw up some dust, the faded red ATV still rocking after he hopped off. It looked like there was going to be a full house.

This was the biggest crowd ever for the court. It was because it involved the schoolteachers.

The tribal court was the brainchild of Mayor Moses, and Chief Snow helped start it. One day Moses told Snow that the judicial system was broken. It was time to go back to the old ways. Chief Snow agreed. Letting tribal elders decide punishment or guilt for mischievous youngsters was more expedient and judicious than throwing them into an already beleaguered court system.

When kids got in minor trouble, nothing ever happened. The kids knew there were no consequences, so they continued to break the rules and the laws until they did something so bad that they were sent out of the village to a group home or youth facility somewhere. They often returned from jail or detention hardened and bitter. Resources were stretched thin, and magistrates tried to manage things remotely.

If that weren't bad enough, there were residual cultural issues between the outside Western influences and the locals. There was a sense that the outside ways had been pushed on the locals, which was true, of course. Resentment ran deep, and often the locals did not respect the law because it was viewed as more of the same. The irony was that the underlying values of the law were based on the same cultural tenets subscribed to by the elders.

Some state officials supported tribal courts, but others in government were opposed. The state was never going to just hand over the reins or cede its judicial authority. Snow, Mayor Moses and the village elders got tired of waiting; they went ahead anyway, without any formal approval or authority.

"Easier to ask forgiveness than permission," the mayor had said.

Since the start of this tribal court, when the kids got in trouble they had to appear before three elder judges. And the kids sure seemed to listen as the wise elders admonished them. They made the offenses personal; the talked about family, culture, tradition and honor. Committing a crime was dishonoring one's people.

Some kids still got in trouble occasionally, but they generally did not get in big trouble. Most stayed out of trouble to avoid disappointing the elders.

This case was different. There was a shit-storm brewing between the teachers and some of the villagers who did not like what they were teaching. This was an issue stemming from the old days when Native kids were not allowed to speak the Native language in school and were punished if they did. Many in the village thought the teachers did not respect the Native ways. All of the teachers were non-Native. Most were from the lower forty-eight and new to the field. They lived in teachers' housing next to the schools, a common condition in the bush.

Three boys had vandalized the teachers' houses with the tacit approval of many of the villagers. The kids were accused of vandalism and Chief Snow was asked to arrest them. He deferred the case to the elders court, not immediately sensing that this was a keg of dynamite.

The chief took his place at the table next to the kids—a poor man's prosecutor, so to speak. There were at least fifty chairs in the room and they were all full. Many people were standing at the sides of the large room that often served as a dining hall or bingo parlor for the community. Snow saw Toovak and nodded to him. In the front of the room were three chairs.

"All rise!" Snow said loudly. The crowd hushed as the three judges came in, two men and one woman. All three were dressed in traditional finery. They were impressive in their skins, parkies, and mukluks. They stood for a moment and looked at the faces in the crowd, especially at the young ones in front of them.

"Please be seated," Snow said to the crowd after the judges had taken their seats.

Snow introduced the elders and read the charges against the three boys. He offered the boys a chance to speak, but all three declined. They looked embarrassed or ashamed. Snow asked the parents if they wanted to say anything. Oh boy, did they!

"These teachers disrespect our Native ways. They teach white ways to our children. We ask to change and they don't. Aren't they supposed to listen to us? Don't we have a say in what is taught?" one mother passionately said.

In the crowd, people were nodding and muttering, "Yah, yah." Some said, "Eee!"

Several others raised their hands and were recognized by Snow to speak. All were circumspect in their demeanor out of respect for the elders. But the feelings and emotions ran strong. There were a handful of schoolteachers there, and they now raised their hands. Snow recognized them one by one.

"We deeply respect the Native people and their ways. But they don't respect us! We are here to teach the children because we love to teach. But the parents don't support us. They don't make children do their homework. They allow them to miss school. When hunting season comes, half the school children are out. We can't teach if the kids are not there! And if you don't like the curriculum, you can suggest changes . . ."

Head Elder Kenny Toovak, Nasruk Toovak's father, stood. The room gradually grew silent. He began to speak. He spoke Yupik. At first softly, then with more power and conviction. There was emotion in his voice. His old grizzled head was back and his eyes were almost closed as he spoke in the halting lilt of the local tongue. Some of the village people dabbed at their eyes. Elder Toovak did not skip a beat as he shifted to English and spoke with equal strength.

"Our people have been here a long time. This has always been our land. We hunt the caribou and the whale. This is our life as it has always been. We live with respect and honor for each other and the land. But things change. In my life, I have seen things change. We must change too! To survive! These teachers come here to help us change. They mean no disrespect to us. We must work together. Change is not so easy, especially for an old man like me.

"When I was young I was a whale captain. Like your father, Johnny," he said directly to one of the three boys at the table. "Your father was a great man, a man to be proud of. In my day, when I was so young, I thought we did not need to learn the ways of the white people. But now we must learn the Western ways, too. If we want to keep our lands; if we want to survive."

Johnny and his mother were crying. Many others, too. This was hard truth that Elder Toovak spoke.

"Today, we do not discuss what is taught in the school. You go to the school board meeting and do that. Today we discuss our children. What they did was wrong. No matter what issue you have with the school. It was wrong. We want our children to be good, to be strong. We must teach them these things."

After Elder Toovak, Elder Annie Blue spoke. She spoke in Yupik and was a dynamic speaker. She was eighty years old, but her hair was still jet black. She was spry and had twinkling eyes. She made broad gestures. There were some laughs as she spoke, and the tension in the room was broken.

She too spoke first in Yupik, then shifted to English. Snow thought it was wise of the elders to speak to the kids in Yupik, even though they may not fully understand it. Many kids these days did not. It was a way to show them their language and take pride in it. And to subtly reinforce that this was their language, their culture.

Annie Blue spoke of how hard life could be in times past. Dogsleds, no planes or four-wheelers. Very little canned foods, lots of spam, which drew some laughs. Most of the food was collected by their own hand, hunting and fishing, picking berries.

Gathering wood for warmth. Then she talked about how there were fewer temptations when she was a child. "But children misbehave, even me," she said.

Blue remembered getting in trouble and having to chop wood and scoop snow for the elders as her punishment. She recommended that these children do the same.

The elders saved the day. Everyone seemed to understand their wisdom and left with their dignity intact, their voices heard. This was good. Snow knew he has witnessed something magical—something mystical, powerful and good. *This is the way.* He was as sure of it as he had ever been sure of anything. This was the way.

The three kids accepted their punishment well, almost joyously. They actually seemed anxious to start their assigned service. They had to help fix the damage and do some work for the elders as well. Snow knew that the work with the elders included chopping or hauling things but also included sitting down to hear stories about the old ways. That was part of the healing and the education.

Chief Snow shook Moses hand but left quickly. He had been close to tears as he listened to the elders speaking. He did not want anyone to see that. He had underestimated the wisdom of the elder people. Again.

■ ■ ■

Snow wanted to be clean, really clean, before he met Lilly. He saw from the smoke that Mayor Moses had his steam bath going, so he stopped and asked if he could join him.

"Got a date with that cute nurse?" Moses asked. Snow smiled and looked down. "Come on! Hope you like it hot."

"The elders court is good. The kids listen. Your idea was good, Mayor," Snow said.

"Eee, it's a good start. We need to start doing more with it, adult cases. Child adoption, things like that," said Moses.

"Eee," said Snow. Moses and his father turned their heads and glanced at him for a second.

Mayor Moses, his father, and Snow sat in the tiny *muk'ee*, or "steam bath." The muk'ee was a simple plywood shack. Moses's muk'ee was a little bigger than most, but they were all small. It was about eight feet square and six feet high on the inside, with a plywood floor stained dark after years of heat, sweat and water spilled on it. There were some low wooden benches constructed of two-by-fours. They sat naked. Towels hung on nails nearby. There was a small woodstove to provide the heat and a bucket of rocks on the top to pour water for the steam.

Moses was trying to see if he could make the gussok chief beg for mercy by repeatedly sprinkling water on the bucket of red-hot rocks, heating the muk'ee to a torturous temperature. Snow was dying but refused to buckle. Moses laughed.

"You are not half bad for a gussok!" he said to Snow.

Snow did not say anything but would take it as a compliment if he lived. He put a wet rag over his head to survive.

There was bucket of soapy water and a cool bucket to rinse off. They all three took part in the cleansing ritual. There was a tiny entryway where they had hung their clothing.

Snow felt as clean as a newborn babe when he met Lilly at the clinic. She was there with the gangly PA, who still did not quite understand what was going on. *Good,* thought Snow. He did not particularly care for the PA, who he thought arrogant. Lilly wondered how anyone could be so smart yet so stupid like the PA.

Lilly got behind Snow on the four-wheeler and they headed up the beach. Snow was acutely aware of her arms around his waist and her body against his as she hung on tight. Many passengers did not hang on this way, instead leaning back and hanging onto the rack in back, but Lilly wanted to hold him close.

Snow drove toward Cape Pierce but only went a few miles. Neither spoke as they rode; it was a difficult proposition to talk while riding anyway. The bay was on their left as they traveled south. The water was flat and pink from the sun on the horizon. They seemed alone in the world out here. Snow found a nice spot under a high bank and pulled over. He had brought a picnic basket of sorts—a cardboard box with some pilot bread and other bush staples. Snow gathered wood and made a fire while Lilly spread out a dark-gray, wool blanket and some fried chicken from the AC store.

They did not get to the food because they were locked in embrace, quickly drawn together by an undeniable, primal force of nature: Love.

CHAPTER 9
THE BREAK

Cliff Johnson, Charlie Johnson's mostly white father, had been born in Anchorage. He was the great-great-grandson of Isaac Johnson, the bull cook from the whaling ship *Saint George*. Cliff was raised by his mother and her family. In the summer they lived in Bristol Bay working set-net sites fishing for salmon.

Cliff had learned how to operate heavy equipment and repair nearly anything motorized while serving in the US Army. Later, he worked for the US Army Corps of Engineers to build roads in his home state. Cliff had seen life outside of Alaska and was determined to do better for his family. He developed a taste for material things and became ambitious.

After his military service, Cliff teamed up with his relatives in Bristol Bay, working the set-net site. Set-net fishing was different than drift-net fishing. The drifters used boats to lay out their nets and pull in the salmon, which got hung up in the net by the gills. The set-netters strung their nets out perpendicular from the beach to where they were anchored in the water. The nets were set in place, and you hoped the fish found them. It was hard and miserable work and folks usually lived right on the beach in tents or shacks during the fishing season.

After the season he hung around for a time. He saw that a well was being drilled in South Naknek. They had problems keeping the drill running as it kept breaking down. The contract for the well was from the US government. Johnson used a contact in the Army Corps to help him get the drilling work. He hired onto the drilling crew, putting his mechanical aptitude to the test. Soon he was running the crew. The man in charge of the drilling operation was suddenly replaced by Cliff Johnson. The drill foremen suspected foul play, possibly a kickback by Johnson, and confronted him about it. Johnson struck him with a pipe wrench and broke his arm in two places. Nothing came of the accusation after that. He knew more than the others and worked harder, too.

Over the years, Johnson got all the contracts for drilling wells in the region. He made some money and hired more crew so he did not have to work in the field as much. He had a mixed crew of white men and Natives. The locals tended to stick around longer than transients from the lower forty-eight, so Cliff Johnson hired as many of them as he could, building allegiances.

There was no store in South Naknek where Johnson was based. Most people had their food shipped in or bought food from the two canneries. Cliff saw yet another opportunity. He knew what things he could probably sell locally. The same things he would buy if he could. He had a container shipped up that was loaded with dry and canned goods, cigarettes, chewing tobacco, and other essentials. He opened a small store after the canneries closed in the fall.

Business was good. The next year, Cliff Johnson brought in two containers of goods. His girlfriend ran the store, which he now kept open in the summer. He managed his businesses. People sometimes would not have money to pay for goods they needed. Johnson opened lines of credit for people. He had a big heart for people when they needed things, but he could be ruthless in collecting debts, especially toward people who did not pay him because they were too busy getting drunk. More than once he had to threaten people or even get physical with them. Sometime Cliff would himself get drunk before working up the nerve to confront someone indebted to him.

Cliff Johnson soon figured out that the biggest and easiest money was in selling booze. He could make more on one bottle of hooch than a basket full of groceries. So he brought in a container full of alcohol and opened the first bar in South Naknek, right in the front room of his store. He called it Johnson's Bar, but everybody else called it the "Gin Mill" or simply "The Pit." The bar opened in the summer and performed well. Booze flew off the shelf. Sometimes his shipments were gone in a couple weeks, leaving locals thirsty for more.

Johnson next year added onto his store and separated the bar from the store. The bar was only open in the summer. In the winter, the store would function as the bar. Cliff tended to the bar when he was not too busy running his other businesses. Cliff was running a legitimate business but skimmed a lot. A lot of cash not on the books. And he was not above breaking the law. He had a greedy streak and not a lot of scruples.

When the US Postal Service decided to put a small office in South Naknek, Johnson also got that contract. He hired a local lady to run the post office. He had the title of postmaster and oversaw the operation but rarely sorted any mail or went in the post office. Johnson also made himself an ordained minister so that he could pretend to be a non-profit corporation and enjoy huge tax breaks. He carried the charade as far as performing a few marriage ceremonies.

Cliff Johnson married a local woman, Nancy, and they had two children, a boy and a girl. He also had an illegitimate boy with a local girl in Naknek; she named their son Charlie and gave him the Johnson surname.

The baby was born the same summer that an Eskimo named Frank N Beans moved to South Naknek from a village up by Bethel. He went to work for Cliff Johnson drilling wells in the summer and tending bar in the winter, despite the fact that he did not speak English well.

Charlie Johnson grew into a wild boy who fought easily. After he found out about his father, he became much wilder and more unpredictable. He hated his father for not claiming him as his son even though he shared his name.

■ ■ ■

Chief Snow got a call from Trooper Dick, who had news from the state medical examiner's office.

"Bullshit Bob died from a gunshot wound."

"Really. Amazing. I never would have guessed."

"His BAC was so high he could have died from alcohol poisoning if he was not a professional drinker," Dick said with just a hint of respect.

He is going to make me ask, thought Snow as he waited. "How high was it?"

"A .42 blood alcohol content when Mr. Bullshit decided to shoot himself. By the way, the ME said the entry looked like he held the rifle out away from his body at least a foot or so," Trooper Dick added.

"Amazing dexterity for someone at .42 BAC, wouldn't you say?" Snow asked, not really expecting a response.

"I know what you think, but there is nothing here. You said so yourself after you interviewed everyone. There's no case even if we had a case."

"What about the shell casing? Any prints?" Snow asked hoping for something.

"No, no prints at all, not even Bob's. That is not that unusual, as you well know. The old rifle was the one. No prints on that either. Don't know why we even bothered." Trooper Dick said it like he had personally dusted the rifle for prints, not the lab rats.

"I know, I know. I still smell a rat, you know. Just hoping for something, I guess. Did they check for DNA?" asked Snow.

"No."

"Have them check for DNA on the shell casing and rifle, can you? I wonder if we have Buck Nelson or Charlie Johnson in the system. I bet they both are. If they find anything, they can run it through their database and CODIS."

"I can do that for you, Snow. It's no skin off my nose. I think you are wasting your time. Even if they get something, what does it prove? Anyone could have touched that gun, including either one of those shit-birds."

"I know. It would be a favor to me, Dick."

"I do have something for you on your friend Buck Nelson. I got a report that a big white guy is trading alcohol for ivory. Nothing substantial, but maybe you want to follow up on it. It sounds like your boy."

Snow got the info from Trooper Dick. Maybe he could hang something on Nelson yet. He would have to do some nosing around.

Snow went by the Round House and saw Stanley Beans chain-smoking Marlboros outside. The weather was definitely turning to summer if Stanley was doing a load of laundry, again.

It is time for you to pay for all those loads of laundry, thought Snow. "Stanley. I won't repeat whatever you tell me.

It's just between you and me. Okay?" Snow knew Stanley would never risk crossing Nelson.

"What?" Stanley said. He looked at Snow. His eyes looked like fish eyes, magnified by the thick, greasy lenses of his black eyeglasses held together with black electrician's tape.

As they talked, a red salmon jumped in the river in front of them. *Jumper!* Snow pointed at it, but Stanley had seen it already. Sign of summer for sure. *Bears soon*, Snow thought as he remembered the grizzly attack, rubbing the scar on his shoulder. He still had bad dreams about that. He heard the bear snuffling over him, smelled its breath, felt its jaws clamp onto him. It was a nightmare, but Snow still felt lucky to be alive.

"Buck Nelson trading booze for ivory. Tell me the truth, please. Remember, just between you and me."

"I hear things about Buck. He's a bad man. He got all of Bullshit Bob's things after he died. Bad. I heard he sells booze. I don't know about the ivory. You should talk to Peetook Tooksook upriver. You should talk to him. He might know. Talk to my brother, Frank."

"Already tried once, but guess it's worth another shot," Snow said.

■ ■ ■

Snow found Frank N Beans at his mother's place, a gray, bare, wood-frame house. Frank sat out back on a homemade wooden bench designed to hang gill nets they used for fishing salmon. On the ground was a long lead line he was hanging with light green net. The green reedy grass was knee high already. The local people had found ages ago that this tough string grass was good for making baskets. Some folks still hand-wove them.

On his short, strong hands, Frank wore light-brown wool gloves with the fingers cut off at the first knuckle. Hanging gear was tedious work and took hours, even days. Frank had a nice rhythm going and continued to work with the white plastic nine-inch needle filled with white hanging twine as they talked. Move the line. Check the length with wooden stick. Thread the needle back and forth through five net diamonds. Adjust the twine to hang out the right length. Then half hitch, jerk tight, half hitch, jerk tight, reverse half hitch double jerk tight. Repeat the process into infinity. Each length of net was fifty fathoms long, 300 feet of tying knots every eight inches or so.

Frank had been living in Togiak for only about ten years. Originally he was born in a three-room cabin in Aniak, up by Bethel. He had five brothers and three sisters, five half-brothers, and one half-sister. The wooden cabin had been very full, especially in the winter. His family was Yupik Eskimo. They lived by subsistence hunting, fishing and whaling. He remembered his childhood with fondness even though it had been a hard life. He was too young to know how hard his father worked to provide for them the bare necessities. He remembered the thrill of going with his father and brothers out to hunt caribou. Frank recalled the mystery and majesty of the huge herds; how his father made them all give thanks to the Great Spirit when they made their kills; the wide-open, endless, beautiful, wild and forbidding country that was as wondrous as it was deadly and unforgiving.

His father died hunting whale when he was ten. His father had been a hero to him. Frank was devastated by his death. He became very quiet and talked little. His mother, Lima, had sent him to live with his uncle, who was a good man like his father, except when he drank. Things were forever different for Frank N Beans.

He was closest to his brother Stanley, who seemed to deal with the death of their father better than Frank. But, like only a brother can know, Frank knew that Stanley suffered just as much in his own way.

One winter night, Frank N Beans was in his nest of a bed. His uncle came home. He was drunk. He crawled into Frank's bed and began to fondle him. Frank froze with fright. When his uncle mounted him, Frank started to squirm. His uncle put his big, strong hand roughly over Frank's mouth. Frank submitted to his uncle in a mixture of fright, revulsion, and some strange sense of excitement. His uncle finished and left him. Alone, ashamed and changed.

His uncle repeated this act many times over the next years. Frank never talked to anyone about it—never. He was too ashamed. His uncle was likeable when sober but turned into a demon when the booze coursed through his veins. He beat his wife and the children and did those unspeakable things to Frank.

When he was sixteen, his uncle tried to sodomize Frank again. Unexpectedly, Frank burst out in fear and anger and punched his uncle, over and over. He punched him bloody and may have killed him if not for Stanley. His auntie never forgave Frank for this act. Nothing was ever spoken of these things. No one wanted to shame the family or themselves. It was a curious hell.

His uncle never tried to do it again, but Frank carried the scars. He bottled the feeling of fear, dread and self-loathing. He somehow felt some responsibility despite his being a boy. He had liked some of it, he thought with hot shame. Only when he drank could he numb the feelings. And sometimes the liquor released a torrent of tears or malevolent rage. He never knew whether his brother Stanley had experienced the same torment, though he suspected.

When his uncle committed suicide by shooting himself in the head when he was drunk, Frank allowed himself no feelings about it. No happiness, sadness, relief—nothing was allowed. It was the only way to preserve his sanity.

When Stanley Beans moved to South Naknek to start a new life, he wrote a simple letter to his brother in his best eighth-grade English. Frank soon followed. He wanted to shed the yoke of shame that was his burden in Bethel.

Frank had worked for Cliff Johnson's dad off and on for many years. He found some measure of happiness there.

Frank N Beans knew his boss's son Charlie Johnson. At first they had been friends, despite Charlie's hatred of his father. But the friendship cooled some on Frank's side as Charlie became more violent and unpredictable. Frank remained friendly toward Charlie but tried to avoid him or found reasons not to be around him.

■ ■ ■

Snow asked Frank about Buck Nelson and the rumors of the ivory and alcohol.

"Eee!" Frank said. "Buck *anik puck boosh*, yah"

Snow and Frank N Beans went back and forth with motions and broken English with some Yupik mixed in, spiced liberally with *shit*s and *fuck*s.

Snow determined that Frank had no firsthand knowledge of Nelson trading alcohol for ivory. Frank N Beans had only heard the same rumor as Stanley. He also heard the rumors about Bullshit Bob and his dealings with Buck Nelson. He hated the "gussok asshole fuck!"

In the middle of the humorous exchange with Snow, Frank repeated his brother's suggestion: to find Peetook, a guide for the small fishing lodge upriver. Snow did not know him well, but it was worth a shot.

Snow put his hand on Frank N Beans's strong, busy shoulder. "*Quyana*. Thanks."

CHAPTER 10
THE VILLAIN

C hief Snow decided to take the overland route to the Togiak
fishing lodge a few miles upriver. It was the only lodge in
the immediate area. People came in by bush plane, which would
land right on the river. The lodge had rustic cabins to house the
guests and a cook shack with a mess hall and area to relax. The
lodge employed a number of fishing guides and general laborers.
Customers paid a lot of money to come this far into the bush
to fish.

Most of the time, the people of Togiak never saw customers
of the lodge. The owners generally did not employ locals, as they
were tied up during fishing season. The lodge's crew mostly
came from the Anchorage area or the lower forty-eight. Lodges,
canneries, and other businesses would hire young people to work
for the summer. They would work cheaper than local Alaskans,
and it was an adventure for them. And they generally drank little
and caused less problems than the locals.

It took longer to ride an ATV on the trail cut inland than to wind up the Togiak River by boat, but Snow was unable to find a skiff to use and did not want to wait. Besides, he enjoyed riding a four-wheeler, even though it was pretty rough at times over the muskeg and tundra. He enjoyed the solitude and the peace of being alone out in the wild.

The trail was easy to follow and led north and east, away from the ocean and the river delta. There was a huge, flat floodplain adjacent to river. The river would flood every year or two and spill into the flats. Sometimes the river would get dammed up with ice and flood; at other times, the spring or fall storms would push the tides. The land was swampy, and in many places there was squalid water standing in pools. The trail skirted the edge of the floodplain.

Off to the north were the foothills of the Tikchik Mountains, which could be seen on a clear day but not today. The sun was out and the weather was calm, but there were clouds and overcast hiding the mountains.

As he made his way inland, the trail veered closer to the river. A few trails led off the main one toward hunting cabins or fish camps. The cabins were just plywood shacks used for shelter as people came upriver to hunt and fish. There were a couple set-net camps as well, used to commercially fish for salmon using gill nets attached to the shore. Those cabins were usually a little larger and better maintained; people worked the set nets as long as they could make money at it. The fishing season had not started yet, but it was a sure bet that folks had been up the trail to camp. Mostly people went by boat, but people also rode four-wheelers as Snow was doing that day.

After several hours of negotiating the trail, Snow approached the lodge. He immediately sought out and made contact with Peetook, who was an Alaskan Native from another village inland. He was a higher-risk employee for the lodge, but he was experienced. This kind of activity was exactly what the lodge hoped to avoid. Snow immediately felt sure he could break him. He saw it in Peetook's eyes and his mannerisms: The guide was a lousy liar and knew Buck Nelson's operations.

Snow was good at getting information from people. He did not think much about it. It was instinctive to him. Usually people *wanted* to talk. *I simply let them*, he thought. Peetook wanted to talk about this bootlegging business. He just did not know it yet.

Peetook denied trading ivory to Buck Nelson for alcohol. Snow put up his hand.

"I already know about it," Snow said. "What I am trying to figure out is how long this has been going on. I mean, has this been going on for years, or did you just start doing this? And why? Were you just needing a jug, or what? I can't imagine you doing something like this unless you really *needed* the booze."

"Hey, I only did it once. I mean, I didn't even want to, really. I mean, Buck really wanted ivory, and I had a couple heads I got from my cousin. I'm a carver," Peetook explained. He went to his bunk and pulled out a light-tan canvas bag that looked like it was made out of old tent material. He opened the bag and showed Snow a piece he was working on.

"Wow, that's nice work," Snow said as he held the piece up this way and that in the light. It was a small piece of ivory about five inches long that had been shaped to resemble a walrus.

"Eee. I learned from my *appa*—my grandfather. He was a master. We would sit by the fire in winter and I would watch him. He would talk sometimes about what he was doing. He would give me small pieces and give me instruction and what-do, sometimes. He finally gave me a piece of my own one day," Peetook said.

"Do you have anything I can buy from you?"

"Eee, I got a couple more pieces."

Peetook showed Snow another piece similar to the one he was working on.

Snow knew that people needed a reason or excuse to talk. They needed to rationalize their behavior. Alcohol was the main reason bad things happened out here anyway, so it was only common sense to use it as a theme to get folks to open up and talk about the things they did. Peetook *did* need the "boosh." He never really wanted to trade the walrus heads, but he had been desperate for a jug. It had been Nelson's idea about the ivory— the police chief was certain of that.

"How many jugs you get for the head, Peetook?"

"I got two jugs. It was a shit deal."

Peetook was afraid of Buck Nelson, but he gave him up when Snow explained things to him. Snow was not worried about Peetook. He only wanted Buck Nelson. Peetook could get a slap on the wrist for harvesting the ivory because he was local, but the chief wanted a bigger trophy in Nelson.

"Buck said now that Bullshit Bob was out of the way, he could do more business. It sounded like poor Bullshit and Buck were not getting along that good before Bob bit the bullet."

"What else did he say?" Snow asked.

"He said he wanted me to get him more ivory. But I said no more."

"He say anything else about Bullshit Bob?"

"Nah. Just that Bob was a worthless piece of shit and he was happy he was gone."

"Take your time and think. He say anything about Bob? How he died, or anything?"

Peetook thought for a bit.

"Nah, not really. Just said he was glad the old fuck was out of the way. He was tired of feeding him booze," said Peetook.

When they finished talking, Snow left. He had a walrus head with two nice tusks strapped on the back of his four-wheeler and several plastic jugs of Windsor Canadian whiskey. He had also purchased a nice carving from Peetook. He wanted to give it to

Lilly as a gift.

He had enough information and evidence to charge Buck Nelson with selling alcohol and illegally obtaining ivory. Both were fairly serious offenses. Nelson had also made some remarks about Bullshit Bob that tantalized Snow. It sounded like Bullshit Bob grew tired of his partner, the gussok Buck Nelson. Maybe enough even to turn him in to the police. It gave Nelson a motive. But without some physical evidence, there was not enough. Snow wanted Buck Nelson to have a serious emotional event. And he wanted to be the one catch him when he fell.

■ ■ ■

Buck Nelson didn't act worried when Peetook told him that Chief Snow had been asking him questions. Peetook did not tell Nelson everything he said to Snow, but Nelson knew Peetook was weak and guessed that if he had not rolled yet, he would.

"So, what did the chief ask you, Peetook?"

"He's fishing around. He asked about who's selling jugs and shit like that. I didn't say nothing."

"What else?"

"Nothing really," Peetook hedged.

"He ask about ivory, tusks or heads?"

"Oh yeah, right. He asked something about that, but I played dumb," said Peetook.

Buck Nelson was not sure how much Peetook had said already. But it was past time to send a stronger message.

"I need a drink; you got something handy?" Nelson asked.

As Peetook looked around, Nelson grabbed him and threw him to the ground. Peetook was caught off guard. Nelson sat astride Peetook and pinned him with his left hand on Peetook's throat. Pulling his bone-handled Gerber buck knife from his pocket, Nelson expertly opened it with his thumb. Nelson liked to use this knife for skinning and sharpened it frequently. He held the knife point a couple inches from Peetook's eye.

"Don't move, you fucking pussy, or I might accidently cut out your eye," Nelson snarled. Peetook eyes were wide, but he was quiet and not squirming.

Buck Nelson talked in a low voice. "Whatever you said to the police, you better hope it had nothing to do with me. And you better not say nothing about me to anyone, you hear me?"

Peetook nodded.

"If you fuck me over, I will fuck you up, then dump your body in a crab pot. You understand?"

Peetook nodded again.

Buck Nelson folded his knife and put it away. He then slapped Peetook on the head with his big, rough fisherman hands before he took off, leaving Peetook on the ground.

■ ■ ■

Buck Nelson thought odds were good that he would never be charged for the ivory and the alcohol he traded for it. *Even if the cops do gain some traction, things can happen*, Nelson reasoned. *People could change their stories, or disappear.*

Nelson was smart. He was raised in a tough environment where you either used your wits to survive or you got chewed up, whether by the tough kids in the neighborhood or the system. He was raised in south Seattle. His father was a drunk who worked on the docks off Lake Union.

One night, his father came home drunk and tried to push Nelson around. Nelson, at just age fourteen, stood up to his father. He beat his father senseless. His brother, Butch, put the boots to their father as he lay on the floor bleeding. Their father died from his injuries. They were better off, and it was Buck Nelson's first taste of blood.

He and his brother were sent to the juvenile detention center in south Seattle. His brother took the brunt of the charges to protect his little brother, who was two years younger. Because of that, Butch spent considerably more time in juvenile jail.

Nelson was grateful, but there was no great bond between the brothers. They trusted each other more than other people, but not by much. They were hard boys who turned into harder men.

Butch did well in the heroin trade in Seattle and Tacoma. He made some connections in Anchorage as well. Nelson smuggled heroin for his brother on occasion. In Anchorage, he met other people in the drug trade. He also met people who lived out in the bush, like Bullshit Bob Pollack.

Buck Nelson met Bullshit Bob down at the 4th Avenue Bar in Anchorage where he met his connection to make a drop. Bob was with his lady, Nancy, and some other Natives. After the deal was done, Nelson's connection introduced him to his Native friends. Nelson liked Bullshit Bob and his friends. They accepted him into their group. They seemed naïve to Nelson, easily manipulated. They talked about their lives in the bush, and it sounded so different from what Nelson had known.

Nelson and his brother had been pinched a couple times on drug charges. But nothing too serious. Nelson did not get into heroin like Butch did. Butch liked heroin. Nelson only dabbled in the drug trade for the money. He was not interested in sticking a needle in his arm. Heavy dealing and usage could lead to murder, which was exactly what happened with Butch. He killed rivals or those who owed money. It was part of the business.

Buck Nelson learned from his brother's mistakes. Butch was serving five years in prison. Nelson thought his brother had gotten sloppy—that the drugs were the reason his brother was in jail. Not the selling, but the using.

Buck Nelson wanted one thing: money, so he could have a decent life. He dreamed of having a house and a normal life, whatever normal was. He was not sure anymore. He knew he needed money, though. At least then he would have a shot. He would do just about anything to get it.

Nelson saw an opportunity to infiltrate the local booze and pot scene by taking Bullshit Bob up on the offer to work his set-net sites. Nelson literally learned the ropes—the area and its people. What he soon discovered was that Bullshit Bob, and most of his network of friends and associates, were hopeless alcoholics, no better than Nelson's druggy brother.

Buck Nelson made enough money his first summer working for Bullshit Bob to get his pilot's license. The next year, he bought an old Cessna 160 for $7,000. He had seen how things worked and had plans. He could easily and safely bring in enough alcohol and drugs to pay off the plane in no time. He was careful and smart about it. So far, he had not been close to getting caught.

Even better, he had a steady supply of pot and hooch for Bullshit Bob and his friends. That had been part of his plan almost from the beginning. Bob was weak. If Nelson made the alcohol available, Bob would soon be into him for money. And it worked out just as Nelson planned. Bob handed over his commercial fishing licenses to Buck Nelson to pay off booze debt. Now Nelson owned one of the set-net permits on his own, a potential gold mine that would bring him even more money and provide a way to launder his ill-gotten gains.

Buck Nelson learned the fishing business fast. The set-net part was easy to do. But he was eager and soon realized that he could be doing a lot more than that. Enforcement was sparse out in the bush. The fish cops paid more attention to the drifters than the set-netters. Nelson developed a simple system. When the tides were right, he would hang a net out upriver and simply supplement his sockeye set-net catch with what he could catch during the nights of fog or when there was the cover of darkness in May and August. It was called "creek robbing." The trick was to not get too greedy.

Fish and game officers, called "fish cops," set fishing

boundaries. The boundaries corresponded to longitude and latitude lines that could be plotted on navigational maps or put into GPS radar. There were also markers on shore—a reflector and light on a metal post. If the fish cops caught you fishing over the lines, the penalty could be tens of thousands of dollars and even seizing the violator's boat.

One time, Nelson loaded his boat during a foggy night in July. It was unbelievable. The river was solid with fish up past the line. You could scoop them out with your hands. Nelson had never seen anything like it. And the money he made! That year, the fisherman were making almost a buck a pound; he made nearly twenty grand that night. He had to discipline himself not to do it too often, or he would draw attention to himself.

As it was, he was the highliner for the set-netters that year—the guy who caught the most fish. A lot of people noticed.

When some implied he was cheating by fishing nights or past the legal line, Nelson said he simply worked much harder than the local drunks he competed with. That might be true, but local folks knew some *cheechako* here from Washington State couldn't out-fish them after just one season. They weren't that dumb, and this Buck Nelson fella wasn't that smart.

Nelson proved them right in August of his first season. Usually, Nelson slept in the fishing shack upriver during the season. It was pretty comfortable and he had what he needed. This night, he went to Bullshit Bob's main house outside of Togiak. He needed some things.

He also wanted to make sure that Bullshit Bob and Nancy had enough alcohol. He did not want them to get alcohol from someone else. It was like money in his pocket. He was well on his way to getting Bob's second site, which actually belonged to Nancy. After that he would not need them anymore, unless he wanted to get the house, too. He liked the house and thought that would be good.

He came to Bob's late. It was dark. He was not surprised to find Bob and Nancy both passed out drunk. Bob was in his chair in the living room. Nancy was passed out in the bed. Nelson got the things he needed and was prepared to leave. He turned back. He walked over to the bed where Nancy was sleeping. She was only half covered by a blanket. He could see her skin and the white of her bra.

Nelson had not had a woman in a long time. Usually he got a hooker, or a drunken Native woman would take care of his needs. Nancy was older, but he had a strong need. He pulled back the blanket and saw her panties. In the darkness, he decided she looked pretty good. He decided he was going to take her.

Nelson was careful. He checked the door and made sure it was locked. He gently shook Bullshit Bob, but he was out cold. Nelson found some Vaseline in the bathroom. He wanted to make sure he had some lubrication. The anticipation had made his need even greater. He felt like he was about to burst. He gently rolled Nancy over. She moaned and mumbled. He pulled off her panties and mounted her.

Nancy began to wake up. He could tell she was very drunk but kind of knew what was going on. He grabbed a pillow and put it over her face to keep her quiet. She was so drunk she weakly flailed her arms. It did not take Nelson long to finish. He was only interested in sexual gratification—not violence. But still, he took long enough for Nancy to be dead.

CHAPTER 11
THE AMBUSH

It was getting late as Snow began the trip back to town. Summer was near, so it stayed light until late, with only a few hours of darkness, and he left anyway. He wanted to get back and was not worried about the light. His mind was busy working on the case. He wondered if Nelson had truly snuck back that night and shot his partner, making it look like a suicide. *Or did Bob simply shoot himself? Not likely, based on the evidence.*

Snow also wondered about Charlie Johnson. It did not seem likely that Charlie would kill Bullshit Bob, but he was certainly crazy enough, especially when he was drunk. Snow smiled as he thought that Charlie might *bite* him but would not shoot him. His gut said, *No, not Charlie.*

Snow stopped the four-wheeler. He stretched his legs and pulled out a smoke as he leaned against the fender. The sun was getting low in the southern sky over the water. It was a beautiful evening. No wind, no bugs yet.

Snow dropped his lighter and bent over to pick it up. A shot rang out, and a bullet clinked off the handle of the ATV.

Snow dove into the muskeg as another shot rang out. A bullet whizzed by. It sounded like it just missed him. Snow was unsure where the shots were coming from, but his instincts told him they were coming from the east. He wormed his way down into a wet bog, a low spot in the muskeg.

He saw an overhang above a stagnate pool of brown, scummy water. Snow quickly waded in. The water was cold and stinky and only a few feet deep. He slithered under the overhang. Just his head, neck, and shoulders were above water. He was well hidden. *Now what?*

He hid, cold and numb under the water, for what seemed like hours. He did not know if he could wait it out until dark. He was sure that Buck Nelson had tried to shoot him. Snow felt stupid. He had exposed himself. But, the truth was, it was the kind of country that was so wide open that if you wanted to ambush someone, you could do it easily. Or just kill him and let the wolves eat him. If you were out on a boat, you could push people overboard, sure as sunrise they were dead from exposure. You could stuff a body in a crab pot and let the sand fleas do the job. *Or you could stuff a body in a place like this,* thought Snow.

Snow listened alertly. He became familiar with the noises out there. He was sure he would hear if someone tried to find him. He did not want to poke his head out to take a look until it was dark. Patience was what he needed. He fought the urge to get out of his hidey-hole. He tried to think warm thoughts. Thinking about Lilly helped.

■ ■ ■

The sky finally started to darken. Snow was numb and still thinking about Lilly to try and stay warm. He was going to go see her as soon as he got out of this mess, if he did.

He did not think anyone was still lying in wait for him. *No one is that patient, are they?* He heard a noise.

"Snow, is it ye?"

Snow stuck his head out from the overhang.

"Kinka! Am I happy to see you!" Snow sloshed out of his hiding place. Kinka of the Little People was standing above the water on a little rise. He held an old-fashioned lantern. He was smiling.

"I thought perhaps ye was shot dead, Snow. I see you are in one piece. Ye seem to find trouble," Kinka said, smiling.

Snow sloshed and staggered up the slope. His legs were like rubber. He rubbed his knees, trying to get some blood moving in his legs. Kinka held out his hand, and Snow grabbed hold. Kinka gave him a pull, and Snow flew up the incline and landed in a heap. Kinka was extraordinarily strong. Kinka smiled again as Snow got to his feet.

"You seem to show up at the most opportune times. You see anyone around here? You already know someone took a shot at me," Snow said.

"The fat gussok that looks and smells like a bear. He shot at ye. It is good that ye smoke, or ye might be dead. He does not know if he got ye or not, but he left."

Snow checked the four-wheeler. It looked like a bullet had struck the left handlebar. The brake lever was hanging at a funny angle. It started right up and he shut it off. He stood and looked at Kinka, who had on the same clothing as when he rescued Snow by the lake after the grizzly attack. But Kinka looked remarkably clean and fresh for a three-foot-tall representative of the Little People. And he somehow looked younger than before.

"Now what?" he asked Kinka.

"You go get him, the big bear. You know how to shoot a bear. I saw you do it before," Kinka said, still smiling.

Snow thought about it. "We can't do that. I can't do that. I have to arrest him and charge him for a crime. I guess I would not mind shooting him, though. I think he killed Bullshit Bob, Kinka."

"Yah. That is true. He is a bad man. You should go shoot him, I think. He needs to be shot, don't you agree?"

Why yes certainly, thought Snow. *But first a shower. Then Lilly.*

"You ever ride a four-wheeler, Kinka?"

Kinka's eyebrows shot up.

"No."

Snow put the little man on the front of the four-wheeler and started the machine. Kinka had an expression like a child. Snow jumped on behind him and they *putt-putt*ed down the trail. Snow stopped short of town and Kinka got off, waved goodbye and was gone. Snow wondered if he would ever see the little man again.

CHAPTER 12
SNOW

Anchorage in 1980 was a pretty exciting place. Lanny Brady was standing at the bar, drinking a beer. She watched the small spider monkeys swinging on the branches behind the bar. She laughed, beautiful when she threw her hair back off her face. She had even, white teeth, a nice smile, and long, thick black hair that reached all the way down her back. She was twenty-one on this snowy day in downtown Anchorage at the Monkey Wharf Bar. The monkeys looked like they were laughing with her in their home in the long plate-glass cage behind the bar.

It was late. The bar was smoky and filled mostly with white men. There were some women in the bar, most of them Native. The Monkey Wharf was a tourist attraction during the summer months. During the winter it was a working man's bar. And a bar frequented by Natives. Strong drinks were served. It could be a rough and rowdy place.

Three white men hovered around Lanny like hungry wolves. Lanny did not seem the least bit worried. She was wonderfully drunk and feeling good. It was the only time she had felt good lately. She moved from Sitka almost a year earlier to attend nursing college. She had done well at first; she was smart and had a good education from the native boarding school she attended, Mount Edgecombe in Sitka.

But Lanny became bored with school. She met some other Native girls and they started to go out and party. It was a hilarious good time. They hit the bars on 4th Avenue in Anchorage and always had a great night. Lanny was not sure what had changed. Things did change, though. Soon she had new friends who she hung out with downtown all the time. She loved to drink. It made her feel warm and happy. But she had terrible hangovers and her grades went south fast. She dropped out of school after her second semester. Lanny moved downtown with two of her new friends.

Money was tight, but Lanny found out that men were very willing to buy her drinks. She enjoyed the fun, the men, and mostly the drinking. She knew she could not live like this and began to feel guilty. But she also felt young and free. She did not sleep with the men who bought her drinks like her girlfriends did. Her friends got money and gifts from men. And alcohol.

One night, Lanny got very high. The people she knew at the bar were gone, and she did not even notice. She felt happy and warm. When the men suggested she come with them to another bar, she said sure. When she got up to leave she almost fell, but the nice men helped her by the arm and walked her out of the bar.

Lanny only vaguely remembered what happened in the parking lot. It was dark. There was snow drifting down sweet and soft. One of the men started to kiss her as he leaned her against the side of the pickup. She tried to say no but was too high. Next thing she knew, she was down on the seat of the truck. Hands were taking her pants and panties off. She was too drunk to offer much resistance. The men took turns with her. It went fast, and it hurt.

When the men were done, they pulled her off the seat. Two of the men were in a hurry to leave. Cliff Johnson helped her pull up her pants. He stuck some money in her pocket and left her leaning against another truck in the parking lot. Cliff did not like what they had done and pitied Lanny. He knew he needed to leave despite how he felt about what happened. He got into the truck with the others, and they left.

Lanny Brady never knew which of the three men who raped her was the father of her baby. The day the child was born was crisp and calm and pure from fresh snowfall. She would name her child Snow. Brady Snow.

His father was Cliff Johnson.

■ ■ ■

Bill Tuzzy flagged down Chief Snow at the yellow police station. Snow had the walrus head and alcohol still strapped to the four-wheeler.

"You better come to the airport, Chief. I think they might need you out there. Hey, you shoot a walrus? Har har!"

Shit, thought Snow. *I'm still wet.* He quickly stowed the heavy walrus head and booze. He decided to take the truck. He was cold. He arrived at the airport as the plane landed. There was a crowd of people there to meet the plane. As Snow got out of his truck, Smally, who was always ready to bum a smoke or ask for some coffee, was waiting.

God knows what Smally is doing out here, thought Snow. Smally barked, his greasy jar in hand, "Smoke?"

The crowd seemed to have a purpose about it. It was not the normal milling around of folks simply waiting on a flight. The people stood in a group. He saw Mayor Moses, Toovak and the Beans brothers standing in the crowd.

Snow fished out a couple smokes and gave them to Smally.

The indomitable Chubby Libbit was the pilot. Chubby spun the tail around neatly and parked the plane with a flourish. He looked like an Alaska bush pilot, all right. He wore the hat with the scrambled eggs and his pilot sunglasses and bomber jacket. Chubby scrambled down the wing of the plane backwards, ass in the wind.

Snow approached Toovak, who had eased to the edge of the crowd, so they could talk in relative privacy.

"What's up, Nasruk? Fresh produce on that plane or something?"

Toovak's smile came and went in a blink of an eye. His gaze was steady on the plane, but then he nodded at Snow's shabby appearance. "Eee! What happened to you?"

"I fell into Hepatitis Lake when I was dumping a honey bucket." Snow smiled as Toovak moved a half-step away.

"Supposed to be alcohol on the plane," said Toovak.

"Do we have any solid information that people on that plane have alcohol? You know the law."

"No. But people came to the Mayor Moses. They are pissed off and want to search people when they come into the village. People are tired of the booze and the bad things," Toovak said.

"Do we know who is on there?"

"Eee! People with booze," Toovak said dryly.

Black Billy got off the plane and looked anxiously around as he joked with Chubby, who was whipping bags onto the ground like they were on fire. Black Billy was at least half black and more than half bootlegger.

Moses stepped up and made an announcement for all to hear. He said that the village of Togiak was going to search anyone entering the village for alcohol. Starting right now. *They certainly picked a good time to start,* thought Snow. Black Billy was as likely as anyone to have alcohol in his baggage. There must have been a rumor, or someone leaked the info that a shipment of alcohol was coming. There were other passengers on the plane as well, but no one looked too nervous except Billy.

Black Billy was wily. He was from some city in the lower forty-eight. He had many brushes with the law and knew his rights, all right. Since Snow first came to the village, he had been trying to catch Black Billy bootlegging, with nothing to show for it.

"I know my rights. You ain't searching anything without a search warrant. I need to see a piece of paper. You got a warrant, Snow?"

Well, we have a situation now, don't we? thought Snow. *Legally,* Billy was in the right. There was such a thing as the Fourth Amendment to the Constitution and all that. But *morally* the villagers had a point. The crowd looked at Snow. He walked over to Black Billy and faced Mayor Moses, Nasruk Toovak, Stanley Beans, and the rest of the village folk.

Snow knew the law, too. It was called "local option" under state law. Native villages could outlaw alcohol. And some villages had gone so far as to search all people coming in. Although it not clear whether alcohol seized under these circumstances could lead to prosecutable cases, the searches themselves had so far been upheld by the courts.

"This is the sovereign village of Togiak. If the elders say we search everyone for alcohol, then we search everyone for alcohol!"

The crowd cheered.

Snow told Black Billy that he was seizing his bags pending the decision of the elders.

"Oh Jeezus! Just take the shit, Snow! Those crazy old Eskimos will just get it later anyways. You know what you're doing ain't legal! You know it!"

Black Billy hurriedly opened his bags and produced about a dozen plastic bottles of cheap vodka. The bottles had duct tape around the tops. Black Billy knew all the tricks. He had opened the bottles and squeezed all the air out, then resealed them with duct tape. That way, you could not hear sloshing noises if you shook the bags.

"That's it, Snow. That's all I gots," Billy said like he was pissed at the inconvenience. Billy was starting to close up his big, black duffle. Snow stopped him and searched the bag. He found a half-gallon of Smirnoff vodka.

"Hmm. The good stuff," remarked Chief Snow.

"God dammit! That was for me!" Billy said.

Everyone nearby smirked. Snow heard a "haw haw" he knew to be Tuzzy.

Snow was surprised to see Lilly by the plane. She was looking at him with a small smile on her lips. She held out her bag to Snow. He understood immediately what Lilly was up to. He had to search everyone to make it fair, and she was prodding him to search her bags too.

He quickly looked through her bag and could not help but notice some silky garments in there. Several of the men craned their necks as he moved her clothing around. Lilly and he exchanged a sexy, lusty glance. Then she looked down demurely. *What a woman!*

After Snow had searched everyone, the show was almost over. He decided to make a final production out of the already made-for-TV event. He felt that the drama would be good for everyone in this moment. Besides, the case would never be prosecuted, and Snow definitely did not want the alcohol sitting in the flimsy closet that served as an evidence room at the little, yellow, tin-shack police department. Better to be rid of it now.

He waved Moses over to witness as he dumped all the alcohol out on the side of the runway. People watched and cheered. Chubby's face, though, was screwed up with agony. Snow handed Mayor Moses the big bottle of good vodka. For a second, Snow thought Moses was going to take a pull off the jug.

Black Billy moaned as Moses dumped the big bottle of alcohol on the ground with a flourish.

"No alcohol in the village of Togiak!" he said, seizing the political moment.

Frank N Beans was standing close by and had something to say. "*Muk anuk fuck ingsihekjnn touk* fuck shit Black Billie *boosh!*" He seemed to choke and spit out words that no one understood, but the sentiment was understood by all. Everyone laughed and cheered. Frank smiled, showing almost all ten of his teeth.

No matter what happens, this alcohol is not going to cause any harm to this village, thought Snow.

The PA was waiting to give Lilly a ride to town. She told him she already had a ride, and he looked puzzled, like she was speaking Japanese. She left him standing there as she got in with Snow. *She has sand,* thought Snow. Toovak, who did not miss much, gave the chief an odd, secret smirk as he walked to his truck.

■ ■ ■

Snow carried Lilly's bag into her room in the clinic. He shut the door behind him and grabbed her and kissed her on the mouth. She had her hands on his chest as if to push him away but definitely did *not* push him away. In fact, she kissed him back hotly.

"I saw your underwear," he whispered.

"I'm not wearing any," she said and smiled coyly. Snow stammered and she kissed his mouth to shut him up. He put his hands on her shapely little butt. Now she did push him away and said, "Are you going to ask me to marry you, or what? You touch me like I'm your wife."

Snow was speechless again for a minute as he stared into the depths of her beautiful brown eyes.

"I want to see you later," he said.

"Go clean up. You stink," Lilly said.

Snow left. He had fallen for Lilly. *But can it work?* She was Native, he was . . . truthfully he did not know *what* he was. He was a cop, and that made things even more complicated.

■ ■ ■

Snow came out of the shower at the police station and heard noise in the kitchen.

"Help yourself to coffee, Smally," he called in the general direction of the kitchen. He came out wearing boxer shorts and drying his hair. Trooper Debbie eyed him up and down. She stared at his scars and everything else. Trooper Dick was helping himself to some coffee.

"You look different. Uglier, somehow," Snow said to Trooper Dick.

"You living here now, Chief?"

"Sometimes it feels like it."

"If you're living here, how come I couldn't get ahold of you yesterday? Out with your girlfriend? Where's your creamer? This coffee's for shit. You ever lock your door?" Trooper Dick said like he was shooting bullets at a target.

"Well, the door needs fixing, like just about everything else around here. It locks, but if you push hard it opens right up," said Snow.

"Just like Mattress Mary," Trooper Dick and Snow said at the same time.

Trooper Dick opened and shut cabinets, then the old, battered fridge. He found the can of condensed milk and inspected it closely. There was dried yellow milk around the knife hole in the top. It was not brown, anyway. Trooper Dick pulled his lips tight and, with resignation, dumped the questionable canned milk into his coal-black coffee.

Snow told them what happened on his way back from the lodge. He opened the locked closet that served at the evidence room and went to put on a dry uniform.

"That's a pretty nice walrus head. You could get a couple thousand bucks for that in the lower forty-eight. I suppose Peetook got a couple jugs for it, aye?" said Trooper Dick.

"Aren't you going to ask who shot at me?" Snow asked the room.

"I figured if you knew you would have said something. Any ideas?"

After Snow explained how he thought Buck Nelson was getting nervous, Trooper Dick put up his hand.

"In case you're wondering why we are here, things have changed."

"I just thought you loved it so much here, you couldn't stay away," Snow said.

"We got a DNA hit on the shell casing from Bullshit Bob's . . . suicide. It came back to your buddy Charlie Johnson. I got a search warrant here for his place."

Snow got some coffee. "I thought we had no case?"

Trooper Dick gave him a hard look.

"I still don't think we do. Charlie Johnson hung out with Bullshit Bob regularly, so nothin' suspicious about finding his DNA at the scene. But it does show he was there. It's something we need to follow up on. Besides, I would give my left nut to hang something on your good friend crazy Charlie," Trooper Dick said.

"You can't do that," Trooper Debbie said. "Your left nut is the only good one you have left."

Snow raised his eyebrows but did not dare to crack a smile.

"I wish I had known about the warrant. We could have gone upriver together," Snow said, changing the subject from bad trooper nuts to regular police-business nuts.

Trooper Debbie had noticed the chief's bear scars with real concern. "Do those bite and claw marks hurt?"

"Only when he is crawling away and hiding," Trooper Dick said.

"It hurts a little sometimes, Debbie. When I lift heavy things. Like when I had to roll that drum of fuel oil into the back of the truck yesterday to fill my barrel at the Round House. It was kinda tough. It's getting better, though. *Quyana,* Debbie."

Trooper Debbie wondered why Snow was out here in the village. *Why is he alone? Where did he come from?* She knew little about Snow. She kind of liked him and wondered if he had ever been married. Togiak was the largest village she and her partner covered and had the most crime. But it seemed like the one village where there was some semblance of order. She thought it had to do with Snow. He was not the biggest, smartest or toughest cop around, that was for sure. *But there is something about the way he operates*, she thought. *He treats people right!*

Trooper Dick still thought Chief Snow was too soft. *Going Native.*

"I heard about the alcohol seizure at the airport. People are talking about it," said Trooper Debbie. "Going to be tough to prosecute a case." She didn't sound like she was being critical, just stating a fact.

"I could have tried to build some probable cause and apply for a warrant. But I was pretty sure Black Billy would not have anything that would help me. I really want to hang a charge on him for bootlegging, but this just wasn't the case. Keeping the booze out of town was my priority, and, shit, half the town was out there. I had to do something," Snow explained.

"I actually agree with you on this one," Trooper Dick said.

Despite her admiration for the chief, Trooper Debbie knew cops had to build a wall. If you didn't, the work got too personal. The problem with not letting anyone in was it was lonely. The only people you let in were other cops. But getting involved with another cop could be murder. She had learned that lesson the hard way.

Trooper Roop had married her sweetheart, who was also a trooper. Things seemed great at first, but eventually things got competitive between them. He seemed jealous because she got a lot of recognition. Their rivalry eventually led to divorce.

"Are we going to talk all day? Let's get going!" Trooper Dick said impatiently.

"Almost ready. Just let me grab some nuts—I mean, some evidence bags," Snow said. Debbie hid a smile. Snow asked Trooper Dick what they were looking for before they left the station.

"A boot to match the print from the top of the water tank," Trooper Dick said.

Snow had wondered how Trooper Dick got the warrant. With Charlie's history, the DNA on the shell casing and the medical examiner's report had been enough. Trooper Dick was a good cop. Even though he knew there was little chance of ever making a case out of this, he did what he always did—his job.

Charlie Johnson was not as his home in Togiak, just as Snow expected. The house was unlocked, so they went in and looked around. The house was surprisingly clean and nice inside.

They found nothing, and Toovak carried them upriver in his skiff to Charlie's fish camp. They found Charlie outside his shack, hanging gear. Charlie was sober and not in the mood to talk with the troopers. Trooper Dick talked to Charlie while Trooper Debbie took a look in the shack. Inside the shack, in a pile of clothes, Trooper Debbie found a pair of bloodstained jeans.

Trooper Dick bludgeoned Charlie with his words.

"Whose blood on the jeans, Charlie? Bullshit Bob's?"

"How should I know? Maybe fish blood, maybe mine."

Charlie peeled off a glove and showed them some scabs on his knuckles. Then put the glove back on and continued to hang gear, jerking the knots with vigor.

"How about the shell casing, Charlie? How did you manage to touch that?"

"I don't have to say nothing to you. You can leave now."

"If that blood is Bob's, you have some explaining to do," Trooper Dick said. Charlie did not respond, and they were getting nothing else out of him. They brought the pants back to the police station, where the troopers got set to leave.

"He didn't do it, Dick," Snow said.

"How the fuck do you know that? You don't! Are you going soft out here?"

Snow paced around the office but did not answer Trooper Dick. Trooper Debbie went outside for some air.

■ ■ ■

Nulakatuk was a feast to give thanks for a successful whale hunt. The spring hunt had been a good one, with three whales "caught" by crews of Togiak. Each year, a quota was given to each of the villages by the whaling commission based on their research. Togiak had gotten three and was able to fill all three.

Custom determined whaling crews by clan groupings. Each clan had a small flag. When a whale was caught, one of the crew brought the clan flag into the village and ceremoniously posted it at the house of the whaling captain who led the successful hunt. It was an exciting time of the year for villages on the coast.

Chief Snow had been allowed to observe the hunt from a skiff that accompanied the traditional skin whaling boats. The skiffs were not used in the actual hunt unless there was an emergency of some sort. Otherwise, the skin boats were rowed by a group of six or eight men that did the actual hunting. Oftentimes the boats went miles up or down the coast to find the whales migrating up the coast of Alaska. A lot of luck was involved with the ice floes, which dictated where the whales went.

This year was unusual in that there was an opening right where the old town of Togiak was. The ice was built up on the north side of the point, but a wonderful break opened south of the finger. The forces of tide, wind, and fate opened a beautiful lake in the ice. It was so close that people gathered on top of "Million Dollar Hill," the gravel pile near the airport. From that vantage point there was a good view of the activity on the ocean lake.

Snow had watched with fascination as the skin boats followed the whales, trying to anticipate where they would come up for air. If they were close when a whale breeched, they could quickly close the gap and attempt to harpoon the whale. A harpooner stood at the front of the boat. His job was to simply stand by for a good shot if one presented itself. If so, the harpooner would hurl the six-foot lance as near to the head of the great beast as possible. There was an explosive charge in the tip of the harpoon, one of the few concessions to modern technology allowed by the whalers.

In the old days, a seal bladder was attached to the harpoon by a rope tightly woven from the tough long grass that grew abundantly in the region. The rope was worked with seal fat to make it waterproof. The seal bladder served as a buoy. The buoys helped the whalers locate the harpooned whale when the beast came up for air. If they were able to get more buoys in the whale, it also tended to tire the whale.

Nasruk Toovak directed the skin boat for his clan. He was the captain and harpooner for this boat and also the whaling captain for his crew. That was unusual. But Toovak was an exceptional man, tall and large, giving him a commanding presence. The ex-cop was one of the village leaders and highly respected.

Snow watched the boats paddle in the calm, gray water, ice chunks floating in the mist. A whale breeched near Toovak's skin boat, and Snow watched as the boat was positioned. His heart jumped as he saw Toovak heave the harpoon at just the right moment, sticking it in the humped back of the whale, which immediately dove. The dance began, with the whale trying to escape the crews and lose the attachment to its body.

Toovak knew he had made a good toss with the harpoon. He had dressed in traditional garb for the hunt. He wore sealskin leggings topped by a seal-and-caribou-hide coat. In the gray mist, he looked like his ancestors before him. Toovak knew that many things could still go wrong. The whale could simply go under the ice and disappear or die, making it nearly impossible for the hunters to recover. The lines tethered to the buoys could break. The whale could find an opening and make it out of the lake created by the ice. Toovak was tense as he directed the boat to the spot he guessed the whale would reappear. He held another harpoon, line coiled at his feet.

The forty-foot humpback whale suddenly breeched under them. Toovak and his boat were out of the water, on top of the whale near the head. The whale blew, spraying Toovak and his crew with warm mist and water. The blowhole was right off the starboard side of the twelve-foot, lightweight vessel. The boat heeled precariously onto the port gunwale.

Toovak shouted to the crew, "Hang on!"

A couple of the pointed wooden paddles had been dropped and floated serenely nearby. Toovak rose to his full height, holding the heavy harpoon high in his right hand. He launched the harpoon with all his might and unleashed a primal scream.

"Holy shit," said Snow under his breath. *A hit! Dead shot bull's-eye!*

The whale dove and the boat crashed to the water. Toovak fell over the side but managed to grab it with his left hand. He was hauled back into the boat by the excited crew, only slightly wet.

■ ■ ■

At the Nulakatuk, Nasruk Toovak and his clan served *muktuk* from that whale to the other clans as was custom for the successful whaling crew. There were big pots of whale meat cooking, as well as a wide array of traditional foods, cases of soda pop, potato chips and other modern foods. A canvas windbreak had been erected around the site to keep out the wind. A blanket-toss, trampoline-type device had been set up at one side.

Snow and Lilly walked together in the large gathering of people. Most folks sat in family or clan groups directly inside the circular windbreak. Others milled in the center of the large circle eating foods and talking. A group of dancers performed a new dance in honor of the great hunt by Nasruk Toovak and his crew.

Everyone laughed when they represented in the dance how the boat had gone in the air. A dancer, with fluid, poetic movements, imitated the great harpoon toss that was the highlight of the hunt and the dance—even his falling halfway out of the boat. People clapped and cheered at the climax of the dance and also when it was completed. Nasruk Toovak beamed proudly.

Snow was almost as proud as Toovak as he walked with Lilly. She looked lovely, her long hair adorned with traditional beading around her face. People were polite and curious about her. They gossiped about the young, beautiful nurse with Chief Snow. In general, people were approving of the couple, who looked handsome together.

Snow watched Lilly as an old woman offered her some fresh, raw muktuk. Lilly accepted the black-and-white whale fat graciously. As she took a bite of the food, she gave Snow a look that made him smile. She did not like whale meat too much and ate the food in order to be courteous and respectful. Snow also took a bite and nodded to the old woman before they moved on. You could chew forever and make little progress breaking down a piece of muktuk. Snow thought the trick was to chew a couple times and swallow.

Snow teased Lilly, "I can see you really love muktuk. You can have mine!"

She pretended to stumble slightly and gave him a little sharp elbow as she whispered, "Don't you dare!"

Snow chuckled.

Several young children ran around Snow and Lilly, urging them both to try the blanket toss. Snow politely declined, saying he was still sore from his fight with the bear. That drew some *oohs* and *ahhs* from the children. They asked to see his scars and he showed them his shoulder, which had mostly healed. Lilly looked as his scar with interest along with the children.

"They should make a dance about your fight with the bear," one of the boys said with excitement.

The others agreed; there should be a dance. Snow did not know what to say to that. He had never heard of a dance about a white person's exploits.

The children convinced Lilly to ride the blanket. She surprised Snow again. Snow helped her up onto the large blanket, cupping his hands together and bending at the knees. Lilly stepped into his hands with one foot and held Snow's shoulder and then rolled onto the blanket with grace. The blanket was held up about four feet off the ground by an elaborate, sophisticated system of ropes and poles. People surrounded the blanket and started the rhythm.

A successful blanket rider had to have rhythm, much like the trampoline. Lilly had the knack. She looked beautiful as her Native smock and hair flew in the air when she was launched off the blanket. She was very graceful in her turns and how she held her body. She was no stranger to riding the blanket.

Snow began to worry about how high Lilly was being tossed. He clapped nervously as she went higher and higher. He did not remember seeing anyone go so high before, but then again he was never this intensely interested before. The highest toss must have been twenty feet. He was grateful when she gracefully plopped to the edge of the blanket, signaling the end of the toss.

People cheered and clapped as she was lifted down. Snow had never been so proud in his life. Lilly was a hit in the village.

■ ■ ■

After some time milling and talking, Snow and Lilly left the Nulakatuk. Whalebone arches marked the edge of the site. Snow and Lilly held hands as they walked to the Round House. Snow dreamily thought of peeling some of the layers of clothing off Lilly, bumping shoulders with her after as they picked their way. Snow did something he thought he would never do but did without thinking twice. He told her about a case.

"I am going to go upriver. I think Buck Nelson killed Bullshit Bob. But I don't think I will ever be able to prove it, unless I get him to talk. I am going to go up there and see if I can get him to talk about it, make some sort of admission."

Lilly was quiet for a minute.

"Don't go. It's not worth the risk. You can get him on something else. You will."

Snow regretted telling her. *This is exactly why you don't talk about stuff; immediately you begin to second guess.*

He shook his head, but didn't say anything.

"Don't go. But if you have to go, take Nasruk with you," she said, squeezing his hand.

The PA careened up to them on the four-wheeler and abruptly stopped, making them jump out of the way. Snow was chagrined at the pesky PA's sudden appearance and his inept handling of the four-wheeler. *A child of six can drive better than that, and most do!*

"Lilly, come quick! We have an emergency at the clinic!" the PA cried in a panic.

"Let me drive," she said, having noticed his hopeless operation of the funky-riding four-wheeler.

She gave Snow a peck on the cheek—which embarrassed him somewhat, though he was not sure why—before she climbed on the four-wheeler and expertly swung it around and headed into the village at high speed. The PA almost fell off and his long arms and legs dangled off the machine at weird angles.

Snow followed on his own four-wheeler after he recovered it from the Round House. A young woman in labor had come into the clinic. It was her first baby and had come early. Often they would medevac a pregnant woman prior to labor so that she could deliver the baby at Kanakanak Hospital in Dillingham. As Snow waited, it became clear that this might become a medevac situation. Snow went back and got his truck in case they needed a transport vehicle.

When Snow returned, it was obvious that the birth was difficult and they were going to transport. He positioned the police truck at the door of the clinic to make the transfer easier. He was worried about the situation. It was not good to transport a woman during childbirth. He thought it might have something to do with the inexperience of the medic.

Rose Stone walked purposefully into the clinic. Rose was an older Native woman of sixty years or so. She stood less than five feet tall. In her traditional, multi-colored smock, she appeared almost as wide as she was tall. Her hair was a wild gray-and-black tangle. She carried a small beaded bag of caribou hide. Rose Stone was a shaman.

Shamans were not well received by Westerners. For that reason, their existence was not well known or talked about among outsiders. Snow had never sought out Rose Stone for treatment but had seen her working on dead people.

Snow first became aware of Rose Snow last winter when a young man froze to death hunting caribou. He went out to hunt when the herd was about twenty miles away from the village. The wind suddenly picked up and the area was smothered by a ground blizzard, accompanied by bitter cold. When the wind lay down, the hunter did not return. The family became worried and a search was launched. Snow acted as the search team base coordinator. This meant he manned the radio and kept coffee brewing. He was not experienced enough to accompany the searchers, who went out on snow machines. It was dangerous work, but there was no shortage of volunteers when a search-and-rescue was launched. Everyone knew it was a life-and-death situation. Anyone who hunted, which was nearly everyone, would want people looking for them if *they* were overdue.

The young man was an experienced hunter and knew what to do. Unfortunately, he had gone out lightly dressed. When the weather became impassable, he had stopped and built a snow cave. He was found frozen to death a few feet from the cave he built. He had taken off his mittens, socks and mukluks in the mysterious warm delusion that accompanied freezing to death.

When the body was discovered, he was brought to Togiak in a sled pulled behind a snow machine. A family member asked Snow if they could put the body in the police station garage to store until the funeral or "sing-spiration," as it was called. Snow, of course, agreed. He did not know it, but a tradition was started that day. After that, all bodies were brought to the police station, where they were held for several days in the garage.

The days bodies were in the garage were busy with visitors. Snow kept coffee pots full and sodas in the fridge. Women brought baskets of food of all manner—mostly Native foods, though there was potato salad and other Western dishes to complement the dried fish, smoked salmon, seal oil, various types of muktuk and other Native delicacies. Half the town would gather at the station to talk, cry, laugh and grieve. Snow was happy he could help the people, though it was weird to have a dead body laid out on two rickety tables in the garage.

Rose Stone came to the garage to see the young hunter. She

asked the family to bring the clothing they wished the man to be buried in. The body had thawed to the point of being pliable. Stone asked Snow for warm, soapy water and towels. He got them for her. Everyone left Stone alone with the body to do her business. When Snow came back, he saw with amazement that Stone was on top of the body, working one of the arms back and forth. It was a bizarre scene, and the chief understood why everyone else had left her to work alone.

Later, Rose asked Snow for his help. She told him in broken English that there was air in the body that needed to be released. He saw that she had the body totally undressed. He helped roll the body on its side. Rose stepped up to the naked backside. Snow did not see what she did, but suddenly a putrid, sickening smell filled the garage. He quickly left, not wanting to know what she had done to release the gases from the body.

As the village people grew comfortable with Snow, they became more open about the secret and sacred traditions of the village. He knew that people went to the shaman often for various ailments, though the clinic also was used. Snow had never heard of the shaman coming to the clinic. But here she was.

At the clinic, Rose walked right past Snow and back toward the sounds of labor. Snow heard raised voices and edged closer to the door but did not enter. The medic came out. He was clearly upset and even stamped his foot like a petulant child.

"I want you to take that . . . *woman* . . . that *witch doctor* out of my clinic!"

"Is the family here?" Snow asked. "What does the family say? I mean, what do they want? Do they want Rose to stay?"

Snow sought out the mother and father and pulled them aside while Lilly stayed with the expectant mother.

Snow asked the mother what she wanted. The father looked away.

"The gussok does not know what he's doing," the mother said.

"Rose Stone has been midwife to lots of babies in this village. I trust her and want her here. The gussok can stay, if he's nice."

Snow walked back to the medic, thinking on what to say.

"The family wants Shaman Rose to stay. They said she is a comfort to them and their daughter. But they need you too. I know it is a burden, but it may help if she is there to calm everyone. By the way, did you know old Rose is a midwife? I heard she delivered lots of babies. She might be helpful to you while we wait for the medevac plane to arrive."

"She can stay, but she better stay out of the way," the PA fumed, though Snow thought he looked unsure of himself.

"Be respectful, or they may ask you to leave. We don't want that to happen. Just help her," Snow said.

Snow left to check on the flight. Snow had a VHF radio in his office. He talked to Chubby.

"What's going on with the patient, Chief?" Chubby asked on the radio.

"Last I checked, still in labor. I'll go check and meet you at the airport."

"Roger."

When Snow got back to the clinic, the baby had come. The newborn girl was already suckling at her momma's breast. Lilly told Snow that Rose had saved the situation. The baby was apparently tangled in the umbilical cord. Rose was able to somehow unwrap the baby, and the delivery was routine after that.

Snow left to meet Chubby. On his way out, he passed the PA, still in the waiting room of the clinic. Snow was torn. He did not care much for this gangly PA from down below. He was haughty and a general pain in the ass. But his intentions were good despite his self-importance. And he was sorely needed. He looked to be having a human moment of self-doubt, which was endearing to Snow. This was a hard place to live. He empathized with the man.

Snow stopped, went back and stood next to the PA.

"Everyone is okay. Good job."

"I did nothing. She could have died—the baby could have died, if it was left in my hands."

"Maybe. But I doubt it. I think you would have done what you needed to do. Rose Stone has delivered a lot of babies; she has practical experience you need. You have education that she will never have. You could be a good team. You could see this as an opportunity."

Snow wondered if he was going too far.

"She believes in things. She is a shaman. I don't think I can do that."

"You can think about it. I know the people need you here," Snow said and left.

■ ■ ■

At the airport, Snow met with Chubby and let him know about the baby.

"Hot damn! I got a couple cigars. Ya want one?"

They smoked a cigar. If he had not been a cop in a dry village, Snow would have suggested they have a snort to celebrate. Chubby would surely have obliged him. Soon, Chubby taxied off in a roar and a cloud of dust and was up into the sky.

CHAPTER 13
UPRIVER

Charlie Johnson went into town to find a jug. But had come up empty. He was back in his skiff and heading upriver, back to his set-net cabin. He was hung over and hurting. And he was angry. That damn Snow was making it hard to get booze. In the past, the booze was almost always available. But now Charlie was also worried about the frigging troopers and Chief Snow serving that damn warrant. He had no idea whose blood was on his pants. *Shit. I should have gotten rid of them.* But he was busy getting drunk. Besides, he never really thought he could have killed Bullshit Bob, no matter if he was in a blackout or not.

Alcohol was complicating his life. He loved to get drunk, but the consequences had gotten worse. It wasn't just the severe hangovers. He had gotten in trouble with the cops. He usually blamed the police, but at this moment he was having a rare moment of clarity; the alcohol was causing him problems.

He was distracted and did not immediately notice that the skiff was taking on water.

"What the fuck," he said, looking at the water around his feet.

Water was pouring in where the two plugs at the stern were supposed to be. He hit the throttle and got the skiff up on step, which got the water flowing the other way, out the rear. He would have to do something—fashion some plugs out of wood or see if he had any extra. So he steered toward the shore. There was some light fog on the river, but he could clearly see someone waving their arms at him from the bank. He adjusted his course and slid up on the beach below whoever was waving.

Charlie killed the motor, pulled it up and snapped it in place up out the water.

He saw that the plugs were indeed gone below the motor, but he was shallow enough that not much water would come in. He turned to see who was waving at him and froze. It was not a normal person. In fact, he was not sure it was even a person.

"Charlie. Ye be needing these?" Kinka asked as he deftly tossed the boat plugs to Charlie.

It was a perfect toss, and the two rubber-and-metal plugs floated through the air right to Charlie, who caught them.

Charlie was at a loss. *I'm looking at an apparition or spirit,* he thought. *One of the Little People.*

"Did you take the plugs from my boat? Why'd you do that?" Charlie asked Kinka.

"I needed ye to stop," Kinka ordered.

Charlie stared at him, still holding the boat plugs. Kinka wore the same impressive homemade clothing that Snow had seen the night of the bear attack. In the mist hanging on the river, Kinka looked from another world.

"Charlie, you need to head up to the big gussok's cabin. Snow is heading there and he is going to need your help."

"What? Who are you? Why would I want to help that little gussok, Chief Snow?"

"My name is Kinka. I am of the Enukins. And Snow is your

brother. He's half gussok just like you. You have the same father."

Charlie looked at Kinka for a minute before responding.

"My brother? That cop?"

"Aye. He's your brother. And he's going to need your help. He's going to confront the big gussok for killing that man," Kinka said.

"Buck Nelson? He killed Bullshit Bob? Are you sure, Kinka?"

"Aye. Shot and killed him. Snow is going to need your help. It's up to you. I can't do this. You either help him or not; it's your choice," Kinka said. "It's going to happen today."

"Why? Why tell me? I'm not . . . I don't know. Why should I take a chance to save Snow?" Charlie said.

"It's not just for him. It's for you."

"Wait!" Charlie called out, but Kinka turned and waved and was gone.

■ ■ ■

Snow steered the fourteen-foot metal Lund skiff around an old tree snag on the side of the fast-moving channel. The skiff was battered and dented up both sides of the bow, the red paint scraped clean in spots with plenty of scratches, reminders of past collisions with other boats, docks and anything else in the way. This skiff had been well used.

Two small, dark-stained wood benches ran crossways inside the skiff. In the V-shaped bow of the boat was an old anchor with black sand on the flukes, a tangle of bright-yellow poly rope connecting the anchor to a small cleat on the starboard bow.

He was past the point of the river where the fresh water mixed with the muddy, tidal salt water. This water was clean and green, running through cut banks garnished with alder bushes. He rounded a bend. Ahead, the river widened and opened up, offering him a nice view upriver a ways. This country was beautiful but also forbidding, even in summer.

Snow was alone in his thoughts, the outboard motor providing a hypnotic background blanket of noise. He stood in the back, as was his habit, tiller in hand. He liked to lean back on the motor, absorbing some heat and vibration, which felt pleasant. He had decided to go upriver and find Buck Nelson.

It was a gut call on his part, and not one he was all that comfortable with, to be honest. He tended to be impatient at times, and he knew this. He could wait for Nelson to make a mistake; he had done it many times with other people in the past. But he also had good luck acting on his instincts. He did not want to wait on Nelson. He thought Nelson might just move away or get more careful. Also, he was certain Nelson had killed Bullshit Bob. It was not like waiting for someone to drive drunk or make some other mistake. Waiting this time might carry a heavy price.

He was only conflicted because Lilly had said not to do it. She had a point; he could simply wait.

Buck Nelson was job security; he would break the law until he was caught. Snow had seen enough to know that this was a fact. Some guys were destined for jail or the grave, and Nelson was one of those, he was absolutely sure.

Snow was confident that he could get an admission out of Nelson. He had experience talking to people and knew that they would often talk if you simply took time to let them. Maybe Nelson was too street smart; maybe not. Snow felt a sudden flush of heat in his face. *Maybe I am being stupid.* No doubt Buck Nelson had taken a shot at him before. He could still turn back and wait.

Things are set in motion now, Snow thought. *May as well ride it out.*

He had a game plan of questions to pose to Nelson. He felt prepared if Nelson tried to clam up, lawyer up, or deflect the questions. He gave little thought to Nelson's violent nature and instead worried about getting him to talk. This oversight would cost Snow.

Snow guided the boat around a bend in the river and saw a camp up ahead. Bullshit Bob's camp. Despite the distance, he recognized Nelson's burly frame silhouetted against the sun on a bench where he sat working on his nets.

Snow nosed up to the riverbank, scrambled forward and grabbed the bowline from the forepeak of the skiff. He climbed off the boat and tied the line around a small alder. He took a well-worn dirt path leading up the bank to the top. Once there, he saw the mound of gear Nelson had stacked.

Nelson was now hanging gear and did not look up at Snow.

Snow looked around the camp. *Neat,* he thought. Though there were piles of gear and clutter, there was orderliness to it. Snow looked at the small, plywood hunting shack that served as Nelson's base. The shack was small but also had an orderly appearance. *Clean.*

The view was good here. The camp was on the bank of the river but also sat on a rise above the surrounding tidal flats. The small rise actually represented the humble beginnings of the foothills of the mountains to the north. But Snow's eyes were directed southeast, past Nelson, who worked his arms and hands back and forth with a nice rhythm. Snow saw the river winding toward town, the flats spread out to the south and east, the visible memory of the flooding of the river.

Snow looked with interest at the four-wheeler trail that wound away from camp in the same direction. He could envision the area where he had been shot at.

Snow kept Nelson in his peripheral view as he approached and stood about ten feet from where Nelson worked. He stood sideways to Nelson, as was custom among men out here, and did not speak immediately—also customary.

"Nice view; you can see a long ways," said Snow eventually, opening the conversation, but there was not a flicker of recognition from Nelson. Snow knew this was a kind of posturing meant to show disinterest or thoughtfulness. It could also be a sign of disrespect.

"Good-looking camp. Looks like Bullshit Bob had things pretty squared away up here," Snow said after waiting for a long minute or so.

Nelson continued to work his gear and said, "Bullshit Bob never did an honest day's work in his life. He was a fall-down drunk and you know that. What do you want?" Nelson glanced up at Snow briefly. Nelson spoke calmly and without any hostility; he was just stating facts. The dance had begun.

"Bullshit Bob taught you a lot about fishing, though. How to set the gear, how to hang it. How to pick the nets, get the fish to market, get a good price. Everything, really, didn't he?" Snow said.

Nelson stopped hanging gear for a minute, like he was thinking. Or maybe just taking a little break. Snow waited and watched.

Nelson was surely stiff from sitting, hanging the gear; it was long tedious work—hard on the back and hands. He was stocky but did not appear fat or soft at all. He was wearing black jeans that had been worn almost gray. The jeans had been cut off above the ankles and were frayed at the bottom, the easier to slip into a pair of rubber boots. Nelson was wearing a gray wool fisherman's coat with the sleeves cut off about halfway between the wrist and elbow. This, too, was common for fishermen in these parts. The coat was unzipped, revealing a grungy white T-shirt underneath. He had on well-worn and comfy-looking leather deck slippers and gray wool socks. When he stretched, Snow saw that he was a well-built young man.

Nelson had a short, reddish blond beard working. Snow saw that he was not wearing the cut-off gloves often employed when folks were hanging gear, but a pair sat on the bench like Nelson had been using them and recently took them off.

While Nelson was stretching, Snow checked his own gear. He had done it so many times it was almost an unconscious act. He felt over his gun belt and touched the gun to see if it was where it was supposed to be, pushed the butt of the pistol down, which was one of the holster safety releases, and worked the heavy belt up his waist a little bit. He checked the snaps to the gun and on the rest of the belt to see if they were secured. Those motions, although rooted in officer safety, were done with such outward casualness as to appear like a fellow just hitching up his pants.

Finally, Nelson spoke. "That much is true. Bullshit Bob knew a lot about fishing and taught me. But I'm the one who put in all the work. It's hard work, not that you probably know anything about fishing."

Snow turned away from Nelson and began to talk about how he did, in fact, know a little about fishing. Talking about fishing might relax Nelson, perhaps build trust before the chief bore in with serious questions about the homicide.

"I commercial fished on a gill-netter for a few years, did some set-netting too. I did a little bit of fishing; enough to know there's a helluva lot to know. And that it's hard work," said Snow.

He paused, gauging Nelson's now more relaxed demeanor.

"I figured that's why this thing happened with Bullshit Bob. You were doing all the work, Bob was drunk all the time. Maybe you had enough. Or maybe he was going to cut you out. Maybe he had enough. What did he do to provoke you?"

"What makes you think I killed Bullshit Bob?" Nelson asked.

Kinda funny how he said killed, *even though I was careful to avoid it.*

"Well, I don't *think* you did this thing to Bob. I *know* you did. The question is why. Were you guys both drunk and got into a fight? Did he threaten you? Bullshit Bob could be a real pain in the ass, sometimes."

Nelson stood up slowly. He rubbed his hands though his hair and stretched again.

"Nah, none of that is true at all," Nelson said calmly. "I guess you do have some experience on the water, because you're sure fishing, Chief."

Snow turned away momentarily and did not see Buck Nelson moving toward him until it was too late. Nelson slammed into him to, driving him the ground. Nelson had blood in his eyes. It was like a good football tackle; Snow was caught off guard and stunned. All his old injuries suddenly hurt at once. His mind was slow to jump into the heightened awareness that he was used to when shit hit the fan.

Nelson was powerful and emboldened. He had been thinking about taking out Snow ever since he showed up. There was no way he was going to let this fucking cop screw up his good thing. They were out in the middle of nowhere. No one around. Easy to get rid of the body, tough to prove what happened. All this had almost immediately been factored into the equation. Buck Nelson was a quick thinker and not afraid to act on instinct.

Nelson was *all in* now and had already committed to killing Snow. It was just a matter of whether Snow was stupid or green enough to give him the opening. When the chance came, he took it.

Snow rolled, trying to roll Nelson away from him. It half worked, but Nelson recovered quickly—more quickly than Snow. He scrambled back on top and grabbed at Snow's throat. Snow squirmed and pushed with his legs, first one way, then the other, old wrestling moves that usually worked at getting out from under. But Nelson was strong and motivated. He countered each move and kept his position.

An eternity passed in a minute. Then two. Snow kept trying to get out from under as Nelson worked to stay on top and keep his large, tough hands around Snow's throat. Snow forced his hands and arms up between Nelson's and bucked with his body.

Snow bucked once, hard, got a little space, slid his hand down and released his weapon. He pulled the gun out, but Nelson seemed to anticipate his every move and the gun went flying before Snow could get off a shot. Snow watched the flight of the gun in slow motion as it landed a few feet away.

Maybe the gun move had sapped something from Snow, or maybe he was simply losing the fight. Nelson was able to get his big hands back around Snow's throat. Their movements were more deliberate now, a little bit slower. Snow panicked as darkness crept into the corners of his vision.

A muffled *clang* rang out, like someone ringing a bell with a chicken leg. Charlie Johnson hit Buck Nelson on the shoulders right below his head with a metal shovel from the cabin. Nelson rolled off of Snow, dazed.

"What the fuck!"

Snow had a million things going through his mind, but right out front was *Get the gun, get the gun, get the gun.* He scrambled for the gun and had it in his hand. He was on his knees looking at Charlie and Nelson. Charlie had the shovel in his hands and was positioned to take another swing but had not struck out again. Everyone froze.

Nelson pulled a knife from his belt. It had a red plastic handle with a blade about five inches long. It looked kind of like a steak knife but was called a "Vickie," and people used them for working with fishing gear. Very sharp.

Snow was out of gas and still on his knees.

"Don't do it."

Nelson seemed to consider, then charged. Snow rose up and shot Nelson twice in the chest, and Nelson crashed into the ground. But he got to his knees quickly and Snow shot him again in the chest and once more in the neck as Nelson began to slump forward. Nelson collapsed in a heap.

Snow moved forward but stopped when Charlie Johnson said, "Careful, Chief."

Snow crept slowly forward with the gun on Nelson, his hands shaking from the exertion. The Vickie knife was a couple feet from Nelson. Snow edged in and kicked the knife a few feet further away.

Charlie still had the shovel in both hands and also crept forward so that both were close to Nelson.

"Roll him over, Charlie. I got him," Snow said, motioning with the gun to Charlie.

Charlie bent over and placed the shovel on the ground. He rolled Nelson onto his back. Snow looked down at him. He was turning gray and dying. Snow knelt by Buck Nelson and asked, "Why? Why'd ya do it, Buck? Why'd you murder Bullshit Bob?"

Gotta wrap this up, Snow thought. *Finish it.*

"He was going to take it back," Nelson stuttered as he struggled to breathe. Frothy blood came from his mouth. "Didn't mean for Nancy. That was an accident. Didn't try to kill her. Sorry about Nancy." Blood spittle flew as he said his last few words.

"You got fucking . . . got lucky. Pig. I had . . . you." Nelson had just about had it.

"Lucky my ass. You got shot four times, asshole," Charlie said after a few seconds. "Take a long dirt nap, gussok." He laughed like a lunatic; with his head back and his hands on his hips, he howled, "Eee! Good shooting, brother!" Then he looked at Snow with a big grin and slapped Snow on the back, nearly knocking the chief onto Nelson, who was indeed taking a dirt nap.

Snow looked at Charlie like he had noticed him for the first time. Somehow he knew "brother" was more than an offhand remark.

"What? How?" Snow stammered.

"Kinka," Charlie said.

Both men had subconsciously heard a boat motor approaching, but the sound didn't register with all the stuff going on. Now that the motor had stopped, they both looked toward the bank. Nasruk Toovak approached holding out a shotgun aimed at the ground, ready to bring it up.

"It's okay, Nasruk. He's dead," Snow said. He noticed then that he was still holding his gun, which he now shakily holstered.

"What happened?" Toovak asked Snow, keeping a weather eye on Charlie.

Snow's voice was raspy and he felt his throat with his hand.

"Came up to confront Buck. But he got the drop on me and we were on the ground fighting. I was losing. Charlie hit him with a shovel and knocked him off me. Buck charged me with a knife and I shot him three or four times. Before he died he confessed to killing Bullshit Bob. He also said he was sorry about killing Nancy. Charlie saved my life. Nelson was choking me out—not sure I could stop him."

Toovak lowered the shotgun and held it in his right hand.

"How'd you get here? I mean, how'd you know?" Snow asked Toovak.

"Your girlfriend, Lilly, got me on the radio. She's persistent."

■ ■ ■

Snow stood in the waiting room of Chubby Libbit's Flying Service. He looked around the shabby waiting area as he wondered what to do next. He felt numb and lost. Buck Nelson's death and his own near-death experience had not had a chance to sink in at all. There had been the business of getting the body moved, getting it flown to Dillingham and all that. Then the statements to troopers Dick and Debbie. It seemed like days since he had slept, and he suddenly felt exhausted. He came here to catch a flight back to Togiak, but right now he was sure of nothing.

It was just about dark outside, and he thought he might be too late to go today.

He went outside, fished around for a smoke and lit one up. He was surprised to see snowflakes drifting down from the heavens. It was almost summer, but it was snowing anyway. He gazed up at the streetlight in wonder as the snowflakes fluttered in the light.

Where do I belong? Snow thought. *Where do I go? I want to go home, but where's that? I don't belong out here, but I sure as hell don't belong in the city. Not anymore. Not after all this. I'm lost.*

He noticed a woman wearing a lovely, dark Eskimo parka, the kind with the colorful fringe at the bottom and a long wolf ruff around the bottom, sleeves, and hood. The parka was beautiful and a work of art. She had the hood up as she walked toward him out of the near darkness. He was in kind of a daze.

Lilly took her hood off and walked right into Snow's arms. They embraced.

They were quiet for a minute. "I should have listened to you, Lilly," Snow said. "You were right. I should have waited. I almost got myself killed."

Snow was waiting for her to say something, but she was quiet.

"I love you, Lilly Wasillie."

Lilly looked up at Snow.

"I love you too, Brady. Brady Snow," she said, and they kissed. "Come home now." She took him by the hand and led him into the night.

CPSIA information can be obtained
at www.ICGtesting.com
Printed in the USA
BVHW07s1412081018
529574BV00005B/752/P